THE
SEVENTH
TOWER

THE FALL

THE SEVENTH TOWER

THE FALL

HarperCollins *Children's Books*

First published in the USA by Scholastic Inc 2000
First published in Great Britain by HarperCollins *Children's Books* 2008
HarperCollins *Children's Books* is a division of HarperCollins*Publishers* Ltd,
77-85 Fulham Palace Road, Hammersmith, London W6 8JB

www.harpercollinschildrensbooks.co.uk

www.garthnix.co.uk

1

The Seventh Tower : The Fall
Copyright © 2000 Lucasfilm Ltd. & TM. All rights reserved.
Used Under Authorisation.

Garth Nix asserts the moral right to be identified as the author of this work.

ISBN-13 978 0 00 726119 2
ISBN-10 0 00 726119 5

Printed and bound in England by
Clays Ltd, St Ives plc

Mixed Sources
Product group from well-managed
forests and other controlled sources
www.fsc.org Cert no. SW-COC-1806
© 1996 Forest Stewardship Council

FSC is a non-profit international organisation established to promote the
responsible management of the world's forests. Products carrying the FSC
label are independently certified to assure consumers that they come
from forests that are managed to meet the social, economic and
ecological needs of present and future generations.

Find out more about HarperCollins and the environment at
www.harpercollins.co.uk/green

To my family and friends, with a particular thank you to David Levithan, a very important architect in the building of the Seventh Tower.

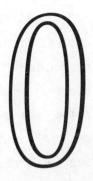

Tal stretched out his hand and pulled himself up on to the next out-thrust spike of the Tower. He stopped there to get his breath and looked down the Red Tower, down to the twinkling lights that outlined the main buildings of the Castle. They were far below, a height that made Tal dizzy. He quickly looked back up.

The wind was much stronger than Tal had expected. It howled around the Red Tower and then spun through the other six Towers before coming back at him even stronger than before. It was also getting colder, making the climb even more difficult. Tal's Sunstone kept the worst of the chill at bay.

It had taken Tal two hours to climb to his current resting place – a hard climb, up through the spikes, gargoyles and encrustations that covered the Tower. Now he was only four stretches below the point where the Tower appeared to suddenly end, meeting the lid of total blackness that lay across the sky.

This was the Veil, the strange barrier that kept the whole world in darkness, turning back the light of the sun.

Not that it was completely dark around Tal. Like most of the Castle, the Red Tower was lit with small Sunstones fixed into the walls and ceilings. The light from those Sunstones spilled out of the windows, so Tal could see where to climb. The other six Towers blazed with light, too, brilliant shafts crisscrossing the sky.

The light made many shadows flicker outside. Every gargoyle and decorative flange cast a shadow, dark against the ochre red of the Tower. There was Tal's own shadow, too. Like all the Chosen of the Castle, Tal's shadow did not echo the shape of his body. The shadow that moved with him flowed and changed. Sometimes it had the general shape of a thirteen-year-old boy; sometimes it looked like a cat, or a two-headed Corvile, or something so fluid it was indescribable.

For Tal's shadow was not the one he had been born with. It was a shadowguard, a magical being from the spirit realm of Aenir. It had been bound to Tal when he was born, replacing his natural shadow, and was commanded to guard and help him. This was just as well, Tal thought. It was bad enough seeing his gangly limbs and scraggly hair in the mirror; he was relieved not to have a shadow of them following him around.

The shadowguard didn't show that Tal was shorter than most of the other boys his age. Or his slightly crooked smile that he thought made him look a bit slow. No one else did, but it mattered to Tal. He'd practise smiling in the mirror for hours, trying to straighten that curl on the left-hand side.

He didn't mind that the shadowguard was only one of the weakest spirits from Aenir, a child's servant. When Tal turned thirteen and three-quarters in two months' time, he would enter Aenir himself and bind a real Spiritshadow to serve him.

If he was able to enter Aenir. Tal clutched the small Sunstone on the silver chain around his neck, feeling its warmth enter his chilled hands. To enter Aenir he needed a Primary Sunstone. Not just for himself, but also for his mother and for his younger brother and sister.

Since his mother was very sick and his father and their family's Sunstone had disappeared mysteriously, it had suddenly become Tal's responsibility to look after the family. He wasn't prepared for this – but he didn't have a choice. He had to push his fear deep inside himself and keep it there. He had to be strong, even if he didn't know where to find that strength.

He wanted his father back. He wanted his mother well. But both would be lost to him forever if he failed now.

In order to save his family, he had to get a new Sunstone. A powerful one, not the child's stone he wore at his throat. Tal drew a deep breath and slipped the stone back under his shirt. He had to climb further. Past the Veil. Out into the full sunlight.

He'd seen sunlight before, of course. He'd seen it many times in Aenir, the spirit world. But it was softer there, less bright. Tal had only seen the true sun once. When he was ten, his class was taken up beyond the Veil and shown the Sunstones growing in silver nets that hung from the Towers. It had been overcast, but even then all the children had needed their shadowguards to cloak their eyes. Sunstones might capture the light of the sun, but even the most powerful could not compare to its strength and brilliance.

Back then, they'd climbed up the stairs inside the Orange Tower. Tal had never thought that one day he would be climbing the outside of one of the Towers... to *steal* a Sunstone.

"To steal a Sunstone," he repeated to himself. It was the last resort, the only thing he could think of that would save him and his family. He'd tried everything else.

It was also the riskiest thing he could imagine. It was a hard climb just to get where he was, but that was nothing. On the other side of the Veil, there would be guards and traps – powerful

Spiritshadows that could chew up his shadowguard in a second and capture Tal. There could even be other Chosen, members of the Red Order, who would be only too pleased to catch a boy of the rival Orange Order. It would be the Hall of Nightmares for him then, or worse, and disaster for the family…

Tal shook his head and started to climb again. He reached a gargoyle just below the Veil and almost against his will crouched down to delay reaching the darkness that brooded above his head. It was almost like being underwater and looking up, thought Tal, except into darkness rather than light. Finally, he stretched his hand up into the Veil and shivered as it disappeared. But he could still feel it. It was still there.

Tal stood up. Instantly, he was caught in total darkness. He started to breathe hard, his lungs seeming to shrivel. He couldn't get enough air! The darkness was sucking the air out of him.

He ducked back into the comfortable twilight and the bright beams from the Towers, his hand clutched around his now blazing Sunstone. Tal quickly focused upon it and the light dimmed. He didn't want to attract attention. Only a moment after his Sunstone dimmed, a faint cry echoed up from below. For a second Tal, thought he'd been discovered and he shrank back against the Tower wall. Then he realised that it hadn't been the shout of a guard, or the high-pitched, inhuman scream of a Spiritshadow. It sounded more like a cry for help.

It came again, and Tal felt his stomach go hollow and strange. He knew that voice! Quickly, he looked down. There, a good two hundred stretches below, was the flicker of a white shirt touched with orange. It was the same sort of shirt that Tal wore, a child's uniform of white, the collar and cuffs bearing the colour of his Order. Someone had followed him.

It had to be his younger brother, Gref, a nine-year-old desperado who tried to do everything his older brother did. Tal recognised the voice and the small, feeble Sunstone.

"If you touch me, Tal will blast you into bits! Get away! Get—"

Gref's voice was suddenly cut off. For an

instant, Tal thought his brother had fallen and his own heart seemed to stop.

But Gref hadn't fallen. He had been picked up by a huge Spiritshadow, one with the flickering shape of a Borzog, a creature long extinct in the flesh. It was easily four stretches tall and enormously broad-shouldered. Its arms trailed below its knees and the two tusks in its lower jaw were the size of Tal's hands. In the light from the Tower, it rippled in shades of darkness, a thing of soft edges and blurred lines.

It had Gref under one arm and had pulled Gref's shadowguard over his face like a gag. There was no sign of the Chosen the Spiritshadow was bound to. But whoever it served, it was taking Gref back down the Tower, probably to the balcony far below, where Tal had started his climb.

Tal hesitated. He wanted to rescue Gref, but he knew he'd just get caught as well. That wouldn't help either of them, or the family. As before, his only chance lay upwards, with the Sunstones.

Tal faced the Veil once more. He'd made a mistake going into it slowly before. This time the thing to do was to reach up, get a handhold and climb through as quickly as possible.

He took several deep breaths and stood up fast, with his hands outstretched above his head. His knuckles grazed stone, and then he felt something he could hold on to. A moment later, his head entered the Veil.

Once again, there was total darkness. But now, Tal was prepared for it. He pulled himself up on to the next gargoyle and thrust his hand up for another handhold. He found one, climbed again and then repeated the process.

He still hadn't come out of the Veil and his breath was going. Hesitantly, he took a small breath. It worked, but his fear of not being able to breathe was soon replaced by another terror. What if he was lost in the Veil? Maybe it was impossible to climb through it, except inside one of the towers. Maybe he was trapped inside the Veil forever!

He climbed faster, not caring that his hands were scratched and his knees bruised. Several times he almost fell, but even that didn't scare him as much as staying inside the Veil. He had to get out.

Suddenly, he broke out into the exact opposite of darkness. Tal screamed as the searing light of the sun hit his eyes. Again, he almost fell, but his shadowguard was already weaving itself across his head, shading his eyes with its strange substance that could be as light as air, as flowing as water or as solid as human flesh.

Tal hung on, half in the Veil, half out, as the burning slowly disappeared from his eyes. He could feel his shadowguard on his forehead and the unfamiliar heat of the sun on his cheeks.

Slowly, Tal opened his eyes and looked around. There was a patch of blue sky directly above him, strange and unfriendly compared to the soft darkness of the sky under the Veil. Around this patch of blue there were puffy grey clouds, some already drifting down through the Veil, bringing a promise of snow. Right in the centre of the blue was the sun, so bright he could not look directly at it. It felt dangerous, giving off so much light and heat that Tal felt as if he might suddenly burst into flame.

The Red Tower, like all the others, continued to soar up into the sky. But now, instead of gargoyles and spikes and carvings, the Tower walls were covered in long, protruding bronze rods as thick around as Tal's middle. Most of the rods had nets of silver mesh hanging from them.

And in those nets there were Sunstones. Tal knew that Sunstones grew from small jewels brought back from Aenir, the spirit realm, but he had not yet been taught how they were prepared.

Tal didn't want to know either. Not now. All he wanted to do was climb up further, because the most powerful stones would be higher up.

Slowly, he eased himself out of the Veil and crouched on the stone ledge, staying as close to the wall as possible. He couldn't see any Spiritshadows or other Chosen. There was a half balcony further up, though, and someone could easily be standing there, or on the walkway that went right around the top of the Tower, a hundred stretches above him.

"Shadowguard, shadowguard, weave me a cloak as red as the Tower," Tal whispered. At the same time, he concentrated on his Sunstone so it shone with the same red colour as the Tower walls. He felt the shadowguard moving and saw a long, thin finger of darkness stretch across and touch the stone. Instantly, the colour of the stone bled into the shadow, until it was red as well. Then Tal felt the shadowguard spreading itself across his back and down to his ankles.

In a few seconds, Tal was covered in a hooded cloak exactly the same red as the Tower walls. As long as he climbed up slowly and didn't make too much noise, he would be almost invisible.

Carefully, he started to climb. The bronze rods were slippery, not as easy to grasp as the stone outcrops below, but they were closer together. Tal could use them like steps, moving around the Tower as he climbed.

He was almost to the balcony, when he looked up and saw a hideous head staring over the railing, directly at him. It was a Spiritshadow head, grotesque and scary, with multiple eyes and a mouth that stretched the full width of its face, lined with endless rows of small but very sharp teeth. It was one of the largest Spiritshadows Tal had ever seen. This meant it was one of the most powerful. Far too powerful to be in the service of one of the Red, for they were the weakest of the Orders.

Tal froze, hoping it hadn't seen him.

He stayed frozen for what seemed like minutes. Clouds crossed the sun overhead and suddenly it was much darker, making the Spiritshadow harder to see. Tal kept absolutely still, hardly breathing. His heart sounded loud, so loud he was sure the Spiritshadow could hear it.

Then it started to snow. Snowflakes began to drift down, only to be caught by the wind around the Towers and whipped sideways in sudden flurries.

Tal knew what snow was. He'd seen it many times through the triple-glazed windows of the Outer Walk. But he'd never been outside the Castle before. He'd never felt snow.

A snowflake landed on Tal's nose, cold and then suddenly wet.

He sneezed.

The Spiritshadow up above hissed and leaned over the rail. Tal held his breath, but it was too late. It had seen him. It leaned over still further, revealing a body like a snake's, all long, smooth and twisting. For a second, Tal thought it was going to fall over, but the Spiritshadow slowly uncoiled down towards him. Its eyes, black points darker than the rest of its Shadowflesh, were firmly fixed on him.

Tal fought the feeling that it would capture him and he would be taken before the Lumenor of the Red and then to the Hall of Nightmares. He would never gain a Primary Sunstone and would all too soon be cast down to join the ranks of the Underfolk. From there, he would be unable to help his mother, or Gref, or Kusi.

The Spiritshadow didn't try to grab him, though. It suddenly shot forwards, and its toothy maw opened large enough to take Tal's head off in a single bite.

Tal's shadowguard pushed him over as the Spiritshadow struck. Despite his shock, Tal instinctively grabbed a rod and locked his legs around it.

Upside down, Tal stared up as the creature pulled itself back for another strike. His own shadowguard was letting out a shrill whistle, its warning sign, as it turned itself into a boy-sized shadow and pushed Tal away.

Tal pulled himself out along the bronze rod towards the Sunstone nets. He couldn't believe what was happening. Spiritshadows couldn't hurt one of the Chosen!

The Spiritshadow laughed, a horrible, high-pitched cackle that cut through Tal's shock and made him swing himself upright and move further along the rod. Then the Spiritshadow spoke, scaring Tal even more. Spiritshadows could speak, unlike the shadowguards, but they never did so in public. They only spoke to their Masters, in private.

"Seek not the treasures of the sun," said the Spiritshadow, its voice like fingernails dragged down stone. "I am the Keeper and none may pass here, save those who know the Words."

"Words?" muttered Tal as he frantically tried to get further away. He didn't know any Words, not ones that might work here. He'd never heard of the Keeper. Surely its Master would look over the balcony soon and stop it!

The Spiritshadow coiled itself completely around the other end of the bronze rod that Tal was sliding on. Tal's shadowguard balanced behind him, in the shape of a four-legged creature with claws and lots of teeth. It would try to guard him, but Tal knew it was too small and weak to slow the Spiritshadow for more than a few seconds.

Tal looked back at it and felt the panic rise in him again.

The snake Spiritshadow shrieked and slowly wound itself forwards another stretch. It seemed in no hurry to get to Tal, though its mouth was working backwards and forwards, almost as if it were chewing.

"Help!" screamed Tal, his open mouth collecting a few snowflakes. He didn't care who came now, or how long he might be sentenced to spend in the Hall of Nightmares, or if he would be instantly demoted to the Underfolk. Anything would be better than facing the creature that was inching towards him.

"Help!"

"The Towers are silent, save for thee and me," said

the Spiritshadow. It arched its long body forwards in a sudden movement that sent Tal leaping into one of the nets. Frantically, he tried to stand up, but all he could do was roll around.

One of his feet broke through the mesh and caught fast, sending a small shower of Sunstones falling through the hole. Tal bent forwards and tried to free his foot, ignoring the Sunstones that were everywhere around him.

He'd just got it free when the Spiritshadow struck. Tal flinched and gasped, but he was not the target. His shadowguard squealed as the thing's mouth closed on it. Instantly, it lost its cat shape and began to change shape so quickly that Tal couldn't keep track. It was a Morlyx, a boy, a Toppet, a bird-headed monster, all sorts of shapes and sizes. No matter what it changed into it couldn't get free of those terrible teeth and the grinding jaws. Finally, the Spiritshadow tossed it aside and it hung off the net, a formless lump of shadow.

Tal bit back a sob. His shadowguard had always been with him, always at his heels. It had saved him from troubles both large and small. Now it had been destroyed in a few seconds.

He couldn't believe this was happening. Spiritshadows didn't damage shadowguards. They couldn't hurt the Chosen. Unless, he thought suddenly, all the rules were different beyond the Veil...

"I shall eat both shadow and flesh," said the Spiritshadow as it reared back and lifted its head high above Tal. Snow whirled behind it like a cloak of white. Tal could see inside its huge mouth, see all the rows of teeth. There were strips of cloth and other things stuck in the teeth, accompanied by an awful rotting smell.

In that moment, Tal realised that this thing had killed before. It was going to kill him, too. It did not matter that he was one of the Chosen of the Castle, a Lightbringer of the Orange Order, a potential Shadowmaster.

As the thing struck, Tal threw himself aside and out of the net.

Falling, he hit a net on the next level below. For the briefest second, Tal thought he was safe. Then he bounced out in a shower of Sunstones, out into the air, too far out to be caught in the nets below.

Tal saw the Tower spinning above him as he hurtled down, along with the snow clouds and the whirl of snow and the Sunstones that fell with him. The wind picked everything up, boy and snow and Sunstones, and blew them further away and further out, beyond any chance of being caught in the lower nets.

When Tal hit the Veil, everything went black. His mind, overloaded with fear, went black, too. He had only an instant before he became unconscious, time enough to break through the Veil and see the twinkling lights of the Castle so far below.

And time to think a single thought.

Why did I ever try to steal a Sunstone?

PART 1: BEFORE

1

Tal's search for a new Sunstone began the day his father disappeared. Eight days later, this search would lead him to the Red Tower, the nets and the terrible Spiritshadow.

His whole life as a Chosen had been transformed one otherwise ordinary day, when he'd been called out of the Lectorium during a lesson and told by Lector Roum himself the fateful words.

"Your father is missing, believed to be dead."

Tal had initially fought back the tears, but they came freely as he ran through the bright corridors and down the Orange Stair to his family's residence. He tried to wipe them away as he ran, ignoring the stares of other Chosen of the Orange Order and the sideways glances of the Underfolk. It could not be true.

Tal wouldn't believe his father was dead. He was missing, but that wasn't the same thing. Lector Roum hadn't been able to give Tal any details. All that was known was that Rerem hadn't returned from a mission for the Empress, down in the deep caves beneath the Castle.

He could be lost down there, Tal thought, imagining his solid, powerful father stranded in the darkness. But he would find his way back. He loved Tal, his brother and sister and their mother too much to leave them. He was too strong to be killed.

Outside the door marked with his family sigil, an orange Sthil-beast leaping over a seven-pointed star, Tal stopped and dried his eyes properly. He had to lead the family. He must not show them a crying boy, but a young Chosen who was strong enough to help. That's what his father had said before he left.

"Tal, you must look after your mother, Gref and Kusi while I'm gone. I'm depending on you."

How could he have known how long he'd be

gone? How could he have known how much those words would mean to Tal?

Tal took several deep breaths, then entered his family's quarters. In the outer room, an Underfolk servant took his school tunic and helped Tal put on the flowing, orange-trimmed white robe he wore at home. Tal hardly noticed that it was a new servant, and a fairly clumsy one at that.

Underfolk were assigned to families by the Deputy Lumenor of the Orange Order. For some reason, since Tal's father had first gone away on his unexplained mission, their Underfolk servants were constantly being removed and replaced by others who weren't as capable.

Tal's mother, Graile, was where she had been for several months – confined to her bed, struck with some sort of wasting sickness that was beyond the healing powers of the Chosens' magic or medicine.

The only things that helped her were light and warmth, so her bed had been moved into the family's sunchamber, a room where every centimetre of the walls and ceiling was covered in tiny Sunstones. It was always bright there and very warm. In addition to the Sunstones, the room had its own steam vent, filling it with hot, moist air from the Castle's central heating pools far below.

Tal went to his mother at once, striding through the antechamber so quickly that the three people there didn't have time to stand up and offer greetings, or get cross because Tal had failed to bow to his seniors and offer them light from his Sunstone.

Tal knew that they would complain later. Two of the three were Lallek and Korrek, his mother's female cousins, and complaining about Tal was one of their favourite activities. He didn't know the third person, a man with broad orange stripes on his robe and a collar of mirrors and Sunstones, signifying high rank in the Order.

The Spiritshadows of all three were quicker than their masters. They loomed up from the floor as Tal approached. His cousins' Spiritshadows both had the shape of a Dretch, quite a common inhabitant of Aenir. They each looked rather like a seven-foot-tall, grotesquely thin cross between a stick insect and a spider, complete with eight legs and bulbous eyes. Tal thought they were slightly more appealing than Lallek and Korrek themselves.

Tal didn't recognise the man's Spiritshadow. It seemed very short and broad, until it reared up. In the few seconds that it took to reach the door on the other side of the room, Tal caught a glimpse of something that had to bend under the nine-foot ceiling and was roughly egg-shaped in the middle, with a rather lizardlike head, four legs and a tail.

Tal forgot about it as he went into the sunchamber. As expected, his mother was there. She had both Kusi, Tal's three-year-old sister, and Gref, his nine-year-old brother, in bed with her, holding them tight. They had all been crying. Tal wished he could crawl in, too, just for a moment's comfort.

Graile's Spiritshadow was under the bed, only its round, strangely blurred head visible. It had faded as Graile grew weak. Once it had been strong, taking the shape of a huge owl, with great tufted eyebrows, and had been one of the few Spiritshadows in the Castle that could fly a long way from its Master. Now, it looked like a melted wax model of an owl, its Shadowflesh light and almost transparent, even in the sunchamber.

Graile was obviously very sick. Her skin was grey and sweating, and she had lost so much weight in her face that she almost looked like someone else.

Tal felt like crying again as he looked at her. He couldn't believe his father wasn't coming back and his mother looked so close to death. Even the Sunstone around her neck was going dark. It didn't flash as Tal raised his own and made his formal greeting.

"I greet you, Mother," he said and his Sunstone brightened, giving her light as was her due.

Graile smiled a little, but could not take an arm away from her other two children to raise her Sunstone.

"Tal," she said, her voice so soft that he had to come closer and crouch by the bed to hear her at all. "Tal."

"They said... they said Father isn't coming back," Tal said, his voice almost breaking. Gref and Kusi looked at him and started crying again.

"Shush, children," Graile comforted them. "It is true your father has not returned, but that doesn't mean he is lost forever. I think he will come back, in time. But until he does, we must all be brave. Can you be brave, for me, and for your father?"

"Yes," said Tal, though he had to swallow as he said it. Gref and Kusi nodded, both unable to speak.

"I need to talk to Tal alone," said Graile. "Gref, take Kusi out to Hudren. She will give you orangecake and sweetwater."

Tal helped Kusi down from the bed, her shadowguard slipping down first so it would be ready to catch her if she slipped. The little girl seemed almost happy to be going to Hudren and orangecake. Hudren was the one Underfolk servant they'd managed to keep assigned to them for any length of time. She had been Gref's nurse and was now Kusi's.

"I want to stay," said Gref. "I'm almost as old as Tal."

"No you're not!" exclaimed Tal. He was almost five years older. "Can't you count?"

"Gref, go with your sister," Graile said gently

as her Spiritshadow gestured with one taloned leg, reinforcing her command. Gref scowled at Tal, but went.

"Sit by me," Graile said. "Tal, I do believe your father will come back to us. But we must decide what to do if he has not returned by the Day of Ascension."

Tal paused. He had been so concerned about the news, and about his mother, that he hadn't thought about himself. He would be thirteen and three-quarters in two months and shortly after that, on the Day of Ascension, all the Chosen would enter Aenir. Since he would have come of age, his shadowguard would be free and he would have to find a creature of Aenir to bind as a Spiritshadow.

Tal had been preparing for that day for what seemed like forever. It would be his chance to bind a powerful Spiritshadow, to show his strength and mastery of light. Deep in his bones, he knew that his father had trained him well and he had a natural gift. He would come back with a great and terrible Spiritshadow. With its help, he would one day rise beyond the Orange, to the Yellow or even the Blue. Tal's parents had lifted the family two levels within Orange. Tal would make sure that his own children would start from higher still.

But Tal couldn't enter Aenir without the help of a Primary Sunstone. He'd never had to think about that in the past, because his father had one and had used it to help the whole family enter Aenir. Now, with Rerem gone, so was the Primary Sunstone. Unless his mother had one...

"Haven't you got a Primary Sunstone?" Tal asked, desperately hoping that they'd only used his father's Sunstone for convenience. Most adult Chosen's Sunstones were Primaries, strong enough to enter Aenir.

Graile raised one very thin hand to her chest and touched the Sunstone on the silver chain around her neck. It barely sparked as her finger touched.

"Once, this was," she whispered. "But now I shall need help, too, and so will Gref and Kusi. You know what will happen if we cannot enter Aenir."

Tal nodded. If he was unable to enter Aenir and bind a Spiritshadow to himself, he would be separated from his family. Demoted, not just to the next Order down, the Red, but right out of the ranks of the Chosen. He would become one of the Underfolk, a servant for the rest of his days.

Worse than that, his mother's last chance of a cure would be lost. The spirit realm of Aenir was a place of magic and marvels, of creatures and beings that had wisdom as well as power. There, Graile might be cured, her life saved – if she could last until the Day of Ascension. It was forbidden to enter Aenir before that day.

"I will have to get a new Primary Sunstone," said Tal, his voice wavering despite his obvious determination. "For the family."

Graile nodded and squeezed his hand, her touch as light as a faint breeze. Her eyes closed and she seemed to slip away from Tal, her face slowly smoothing into sleep.

"I will get a Primary Sunstone," repeated Tal quietly. "Somehow."

Tal sat by his mother for a long time, thinking of how he could get a new, powerful Sunstone. He could think of only three ways and all carried some risk.

The first would be to ask his mother's cousins, Lallek and Korrek. They were higher up in the Orange Order, rumoured to be going Yellow soon. They both wore several Sunstones – in their silver circlets, in the rings that flashed upon their fingers, even set in the points of their mirror-bright shoes. Tal thought they must have won them gambling. He'd never seen Lallek or Korrek do anything else.

But Lallek and Korrek were not known for their generosity, and Tal thought that they particularly disliked him. He couldn't understand why, though when he was younger he had set up a bucket of ash to fall on them, dulling their brilliance just before a family dinner. It had only been a joke, but they seemed to hold a grudge. Of course, it hadn't just been ash.

Still, Tal thought, they were family. And they were just outside, in the reception room. Though that was probably only because everyone would expect them to come, now that the news was out about Rerem's presumed death.

Tal sighed. His shadowguard, catching his mood, changed shape from a two-headed Corvile to an almost normal shadow. It shivered and made a sort of throwing-up motion before slipping back into the long, catlike shape of a Corvile, though with only one head. It made Tal smile. Even his shadowguard disliked Lallek and Korrek.

This time, Tal stopped at the door and made the proper bow to his elders. He raised his Sunstone and said, "I greet you, Korrek, Lallek and . . ."

"Shadowmaster Sushin," said the unknown man, negligently raising his own Sunstone and rudely blasting a very bright white light into Tal's face. Korrek and Lallek did the same, so Tal had to raise his hand to shield his eyes.

The light grew brighter still and Tal felt an unpleasant heat on his hand. His shadowguard let out a whistle, so low only Tal could hear. Tal felt anger building inside him, as hot and bright as the light. His cousins and this unknown Shadowmaster – a title that meant he served the Empress directly, in addition to his rank in the Orange Order – would never have dared treat him like this if his mother or father were around.

The light disappeared and Tal brought his hand down. None of the three had bothered to get up, but their Spiritshadows had moved forwards and were standing over Tal, unpleasantly close. The Shadowmaster's, Tal realised, was a deepwater Shellbeast. It had a flat shell or carapace that covered its middle.

"The Shadowmaster was not impressed by your rudeness," said Lallek. "Even under the circumstances, one must not forget the proper way to do things."

"I beg the Shadowmaster's forgiveness," Tal said slowly, forcing the words out. "May my light diminish no further in his eyes."

The Shadowmaster grunted. He looked like a pig, Tal thought. He had a fat face, ready to grub at any trough, like the pigs the Underfolk herded in the farm caverns far below.

"Take three deluminents," said the Shadowmaster, picking four clear bracelets out of his sleeve pocket and throwing them to Tal.

They landed on the ground, since Tal was too shocked to catch them. He bent to pick them up, slowly slipping each one over his hand on to his wrist. Deluminents were visible punishments, marking an offence against the Order or the Empress. They could only be removed by someone higher than the person who'd given them in the first place. If Tal picked up seven deluminents, he would be demoted to the Red Order. Seven more after that and he would be joining the Underfolk, even before the Day of Ascension.

After putting on the third bracelet, Tal stopped and looked at the Shadowmaster. Three deluminents was a ridiculously harsh punishment for not greeting his superiors properly. But the Shadowmaster had thrown four!

"There are four deluminents, Shadowmaster," he said, feeling his face flush with the humiliation. He had never had more than a single deluminent in his life.

"Three, four, it doesn't matter," said the Shadowmaster. "Put it on, Tal. You must learn to pay proper respect."

Slowly, Tal picked up the fourth deluminent and slid it on to his wrist. The bracelets were made of crystal and jangled as they touched.

"How can I serve my distinguished visitors?" Tal asked, following the proper ritual, even though he wanted to pick up a jug of frosted sweetwater and throw it in their faces.

"I am the Shadowmaster Sushin, Brightstar of the Orange Order and Spectral Adept," announced the fat man. "I have come to offer the Empress's sorrow at the death of your father."

"He's not dead," Tal wanted to say, but he did not dare speak aloud. This Shadowmaster seemed to want him to be disrespectful. He was even reaching into his sleeve pocket to jangle the deluminents there, while he watched Tal struggle with his feelings.

"We thank the Empress," said Tal. He didn't really understand what was going on. Why was this Shadowmaster so hostile to him? He expected his cousins to be nasty, but this man was a stranger, a servant of the Empress.

"That's it, really," said Sushin. He took a handful of dried shrimps out of his voluminous pocket and stuffed them into his mouth, still talking. "You may go back to the Lectorium now, Tal. Must keep up with your studies."

Tal felt sick, watching the huge wad of pink, munched-up shrimps churning about in Sushin's mouth. The man was a pig and a bully.

Shrimps were his mother's favourite, and hard to come by, since they were rarely trapped in the deep underground streams by the Underfolk. Tal had been trying to get her some for weeks, without success.

"I desire to ask a question of my mother's cousins, if I may," Tal said carefully. Despite the anger he felt at having to ask permission to speak in his own home, he had no choice.

"Ask away," replied Sushin. He took another handful of shrimps and washed them down with a glass of sweetwater, spilling it down the deep furrows where his bloated cheeks met his mouth.

"Light shine on you, Shadowmaster," said Tal, bowing again. He turned to his cousins, who were smiling, but not in a nice way. They seemed to be looking forward to something. Their Spiritshadows jiggled in front of Tal, almost dancing, so he had to talk between them.

"Mother is ill," he began. "And since Father is missing, we will need help to enter Aenir when the Day of Ascension comes. I ask your help, as close cousins to my mother. Grant us a Sunstone of sufficient power to be a Primary Sunstone."

Lallek and Korrek looked at each other and their smiles grew wider. Then they looked at Sushin and everyone smiled. Except Tal.

"Oh no," said Lallek, fingering the two very large Sunstones that flashed on her thumb and forefinger rings. "We really haven't any to spare."

"What a shame," added Korrek, lightly touching the pendant she wore that held four Sunstones, all of them twice as large as Tal's own. "But I'm sure you'll manage somehow... even though your father is dead."

Tal stared at them, his fury growing. Dimly, he was aware of his shadowguard gripping him around the knees so he couldn't charge forwards. He gripped his own Sunstone, wishing that he could throw lightspears from it, or the rain of sparks, or any of the other combat magic that he had only just begun to learn in the Lectorium.

Sushin broke the tension by shovelling the last of the shrimps into his mouth and pushing himself up out of the chair. Lallek and Korrek hastily jumped up as well. By rights, all three should have bowed to Tal, as they were in his house. But they didn't. Sushin just walked out, followed by the two women. The Spiritshadows backed away slowly. They knew, even if their masters did not, that Tal was very close to some sort of crazy attack.

When the Underfolk servant closed the door behind them, the shadowguard let Tal go. His breathing started to work again and he could think.

His first plan to get a Sunstone had failed miserably. He would have to move on to the next plan. And he would have to try to find out why Shadowmaster Sushin wanted him to fail.

"You'll see," Tal whispered to the door. He raised his arm and jangled the deluminents. "You'll see. I'll get my Sunstone!"

His shadowguard grew an arm and shook it, too, in silent protest. It kept on after Tal stopped and had to race to catch up with him as he went to see how Gref and Kusi were coping with the terrible news.

3

Tal's second plan would have to wait for seven days, when he could enter the next Achievement of Luminosity. While he waited, he tried very hard to be a model student. Whenever an idea for a practical joke came into his head, or he got bored as the Assistant Lector droned on about recursive light or spectral shifting, the soft chink of the deluminents on his wrist would remind him to behave.

Even with his best efforts, it was a hard week for Tal. After every evening meal, Kusi would forget and ask for her father to put her to bed. She cried when he didn't come, and was too young to understand that it wasn't because he didn't want to. Graile was too weak to get out of bed herself, so it had fallen to Tal to tuck the little girl in and tell her a story. He then had to make sure that Gref actually went to bed at all.

It was all a constant reminder of his father's absence. Tal would lie awake at night, hoping that he would hear his father's footsteps outside his room and his familiar voice asking him if all was well.

Unfortunately, Tal was much more likely to hear Gref's voice saying something like, "Tal, why don't I sneak over to Lallek's rooms and steal a Sunstone?"

Or, "Tal, I bet I could drop a blanket on Korrek and get her bracelet off and she wouldn't know who did it."

Or Gref's most constant question, "Tal, why can't I help you get a new Sunstone?"

Kusi was not much better, in her own way. Besides having to read her a story, most nights he had to help her get back to sleep. She'd lie in bed looking up at him with her huge blue eyes and say, "I don't want Tal. I want Mummy."

To make matters worse, Shadowmaster Sushin

seemed to have spread the word that Tal was to be picked on. Older Chosen he had never seen before tried to get in his way and blame him for the collision. Strange Spiritshadows followed him so often he stopped using the smaller stairways. He even avoided the best shortcut in the Castle: the Underfolk's laundry chute – a slippery slide that spiralled from the highest chambers of the Violet down to the Red and then beneath to the Underfolk's work caverns.

Tal didn't want to meet a Spiritshadow in the laundry slide. Being in the slide was the closest you could get to real darkness in the Castle. There were no Sunstones inside. The only light came spilling in around the hatches on each of the forty-nine Order levels. These faint lines of light were also the only way for chute riders to know where they were, so they could push their feet out and bring themselves to a stop, usually with some damage to the soles of their shoes.

So Tal kept to the main stairs and the Colourless Corridors, the wide passageways that were not part of the realm of any particular Order.

In the Lectorium they were taught that all light served the Empress, that all the Orders were like a family.

Tal knew this was a load of shadowspit. The Chosen in the lower Orders were resentful of the higher ones, and the Chosen of the higher Orders liked putting everyone in their place. The children were the worst. If they caught Tal creeping about, they'd gang up to blind him with their Sunstones, a blindness that sometimes took days to fully wear off.

Tal just tried to avoid trouble. It was even more difficult because he had to look after Gref as well. His brother was in a different Lectorium and he hadn't complained to Tal about any problems. Still, Tal tried to keep an eye on him.

Gref had a genius for trouble. He was very good at making it and at avoiding responsibility for it. But even getting away with things eight times out of ten meant getting caught twice.

Gref's genius did not serve him well when it came to being picked on. Tal wasn't so much worried about what might happen to Gref, but what his younger brother might do to take revenge.

The case of the boy who had drawn a picture of Gref as a two-headed Toppet was never far from Tal's mind. Gref had saved his allowance for seven months, then paid a much older student to create a light-puppet of himself as a truly vicious Toppet, which he'd managed to get into the other boy's room at night. The boy had woken up with a scream they could hear in all seven Towers; he still couldn't see a light-puppet show without shaking nervously.

Gref's glory hadn't lasted long. It was clear to the authorities where the light-puppet had come from, with Gref's face on it.

What worried Tal the most was that even after being punished, Gref said it was worth it – and he'd do it again. (Luckily, he wasn't old enough to be given deluminents.)

All of this trouble was a constant worry for Tal, but it was nothing compared to the continuing absence of his father. If he came back, everything would be all right. With every day that passed without him, Tal's secret fear that his father might really be dead grew stronger.

He had to think harder about getting a Primary

Sunstone. If only the horrible Lallek and Korrek had just given him a Sunstone, he wouldn't have to try to win an Achievement of Luminosity.

The Achievements of Luminosity were held every quarter month and were technically open to everyone who wished to demonstrate their skill and artistic abilities. It was rare for someone who only had a shadowguard, like Tal, to participate.

The Achievements were divided into several categories, each held in different parts of the Castle. While all Achievements tested the participant's skill with a Sunstone and sense of light, each category tested other specific talents and abilities as well.

Tal had put his name down for the Achievement of Body. This Achievement was essentially an obstacle course, where fitness and dexterity were as important as light control. It was held in the Hall of Mirrors, which added an extra level of difficulty. Light had to be tightly controlled there, because the slightest slip would mean thousands of embarrassing reflections.

Over the week, Tal practised on the course every

afternoon after he finished at the Lectorium. There were seven obstacles, each of which had to be jumped, climbed, swung across or crawled under. The ancient obstacles were made of solid light, a magic that was now lost to the Chosen, though some thought the Empress might know the secret ways.

Participants could make the obstacle change into something else by directing a beam of light from their Sunstone at exactly the right spot, in exactly the right colour.

The secret to doing well at the Achievement of Body was to turn all the obstacles in front of yourself into something easy, like a Gasping Hole, which could be jumped across. At the same time, you had to turn your competitors' obstacles into more difficult things, like a Surprising Wall.

Sometimes obstacles flickered through multiple combinations right up until the last second, as light beams shot everywhere. It was not unknown for a Gasping Hole to become a Surprising Wall in the same instant that a competitor jumped, resulting in an unpleasant collision.

Tal wasn't worried so much about that. Getting

knocked out by smacking his head into a Surprising Wall or tripping over a sudden Deep Tunnel wasn't a problem. The audience would just laugh. But any disregard of the rules of light could lead to more deluminents, and Tal couldn't afford that.

"That won't happen," he muttered after another exhausting practice. The winner of the Achievement was usually advanced several levels within his or her Order, or was permitted to ask for a Sunstone or some other reward instead.

Tal intended to be the winner. He'd always been good at the trial Achievements, which all the children competed in. The practices were going well. What could go wrong?

On the morning of the Achievements of Luminosity, Tal found out exactly what could go wrong. Nervous, he went to the Hall of Mirrors a good hour early – and discovered that his name was not on the list for that day's Achievement of Body. It wasn't on the list for next time either or the one after that.

"But I wrote it down," Tal insisted. "In the Registry. A week ago!"

The Half-Bright who had the list for the Achievement of Body shrugged. He was a low-ranking Chosen of the Red Order, better than a Dimmer but not much above an Underfolk, which was why he had an actual job. Most Chosen didn't do anything so menial, devoting themselves to their hobbies or interests, or in advancing themselves through Achievements or the politics of the Empress's court.

"You're not here," he said, holding up the huge leather-bound book. "Maybe you accidentally signed up for some other Achievement."

"I can't have," said Tal. His shadowguard shook its head, too.

"You'll have to go to the Registry and check," said the Half-Bright. His Spiritshadow was as lacklustre as he was, a six-legged animal of some kind that slept around his ankles.

Tal nodded and sped away. Behind him, he heard the man snort something like "Orange idiot", but Tal didn't look back. He remembered exactly what he'd signed up for. He couldn't have made a mistake...

Unless he'd signed up for the wrong Achievement.

What if he'd signed up for the Achievement of Combat or the Achievement of Healing? He wasn't properly trained for either of those. He'd get the White Ray of Disgust from the audience for sure and have his arms loaded with deluminents. He'd become an Underfolk, his mother would die, and Gref and Kusi would follow him down into the dark servant halls below the Castle.

"I must not panic," Tal told himself. He stopped running and carefully bowed and gave light to a Brilliance of the Violet who passed by. He still had half an hour left.

"I must not panic," Tal repeated to himself. Taking deliberate, slow breaths, he walked quickly towards the Registry.

It was the Achievement of Music. Tal stared down at the Registry, unable to believe that his name was there. But it was, complete with his family sigil, etched in light.

He couldn't possibly have made this mistake... but obviously he had.

The Achievement of Music! After Combat and Healing, that was probably the worst. Tal didn't even have a composition to use. He couldn't withdraw either. That wasn't allowed, unless he was sick or injured.

For a moment, Tal thought of throwing himself down one of the steeper stairways. A broken arm or leg would let him off. For now. But then he would have no chance in any of the Achievements.

Tal glanced at his Sunstone, looking at the bands of colour to work out the time. He had less than twenty minutes before he would have to perform an original composition of light and music.

It was impossible. Like all the Chosen, Tal was a trained musician. But he had never displayed any great talent, and he certainly didn't have time to write an entirely new piece of music. His only chance would be to use an old one. It would have to be something that had never been performed before, or so old no one recognised it.

"Old," Tal said to himself and an idea suddenly came into his head. His shadowguard caught his thought and changed from a very ugly sort of lungfish into a thin, stooped man much taller than Tal, with a very pronounced nose. It was a caricature – one that Tal recognised. His Great-uncle Ebbitt!

Ebbitt would help! Tal was off again, racing through the corridors. He had to forget about being careful and took every shortcut he knew.

Two minutes later, Tal was throwing himself feet

first into the laundry chute. A huge bag of clothes hurtled just ahead of him, then Tal was sliding down himself, counting the levels.

"Orange Three, Two, One, Red Six, Five, Four, Three," he said aloud, the sound of his own voice making him feel better. At "Red Two" he stuck his feet into the sides of the chute and felt the sudden heat through the soles of his shoes as friction slowed him down.

Ebbitt lived in Red One, the very lowest level of the Chosen. Below that lay the work caverns of the Underfolk. Tal had never been there. He knew there were few Sunstones in the Underfolk caverns, just enough to create a dim twilight so the servants could work. It was said to be perpetually steamy as well, from the hot pools that supplied the Castle's warmth. Below the pools, tunnels of lava flowed. The lava collection pools were the creation of the Castle's builders, the Chosen of long ago, who wielded many powers the current generations had long lost.

Tal felt a chill go through him as he climbed out of the chute. Soon he might be forced to join the Underfolk, and might never return to the bright levels of the Chosen. Even today, if he completely failed in the Achievement of Music and was given more deluminents . . .

He checked his Sunstone again. He only had fifteen minutes left until the Achievement. If Ebbitt wasn't home, Tal didn't know what he would do. He set off at a run, hoping that he didn't meet any Red Half-Brights or Dimmers who would be delighted to politely delay an Orange boy. They wouldn't do any serious harm, but they would waste his precious time.

Ebbitt had once been a Shadowlord himself, a Brightblinder of the Indigo Order, the second highest in the Castle. Ebbitt had been the shining hope of the family and had seemed certain of climbing Violet. But something had gone terribly wrong for him when Tal was a baby. He had been forced all the way down to Red, and the lowest level. He was a Dimmer now, a single step above the Underfolk. Somehow he managed to stay there, despite his strange ways and outspoken tongue.

He chose to live in twilight, at the end of a rough

tunnel, without a door. His weird collection of constantly rearranged furniture occupied a good forty stretches of corridor and Ebbitt himself could be found anywhere around it. Tal had no idea how he stopped people coming in, or stealing his things. But he had never seen anyone there except family or invited guests.

Today, a large wardrobe of white stone marked the beginning of Ebbitt's realm. It completely blocked the corridor and Tal was momentarily stumped by it. Then he opened the door and saw that the wardrobe had no back. He went through, shutting the door behind him.

After carefully making his way around several chairs and desks, a huge birdcage and a bronze orrery, Tal found Ebbitt sleeping on an old gilded throne. It had obviously once been studded with Sunstones because it was covered in holes and scratch marks from when they had been removed.

Ebbitt himself was wearing a plain grey robe without any of the proper markings of his Order or position. He wore a single small Sunstone in a silver ring on his index finger. It flashed as Tal approached and Ebbitt's Spiritshadow stepped out of the darkness behind the throne.

It was a huge cat, with a great mane around its head and a ridge along its back. Completely black even in the dim light – the mark of a powerful Spiritshadow – it yawned as Tal approached, showing lighter shadows inside its enormous mouth.

Tal's shadowguard turned itself into a smaller version of the maned cat in tribute. Tal took a few steps forwards, but not too many. He'd always been a bit afraid of Ebbitt's Spiritshadow even though he knew it wouldn't hurt him.

"Great-uncle," he said. As Ebbitt still didn't move, he said it again, a bit louder. "Great-uncle!"

Ebbitt still didn't move. Tal took another step forwards and almost shouted, "Uncle Ebbitt!"

The old man on the throne reacted to that. He jumped up and shouted, "Kill!"

The huge cat Spiritshadow leaped forwards. Tal jumped back and fell over a small three-legged stool, hurtling towards the hard stone floor.

At the last moment, Tal's shadowguard shot underneath him, cushioning his head so he didn't knock himself out.

Ebbitt laughed as Tal slowly got up, and the maned cat slunk back to sit beside the throne, at the old man's right hand.

"That fooled you, boy," wheezed Ebbitt. "Thought I was asleep, didn't you?"

Tal got up angrily, but managed not to show it. There was no point in getting angry with Ebbitt. He just laughed and wheezed.

"I need your help, Uncle," Tal said quickly. Ebbitt might be a pain when it came to surprises and practical jokes, but he was a lot more use than Korrek and Lallek when it came to helping out.

"Help?" asked Ebbitt. His laugh was gone and he didn't look an old fool any more. Obviously, Tal's face and tone had told him that whatever the boy was concerned about, it was serious. "Tell me."

"You know about Father," said Tal, speaking so quickly his words ran into each other. "I don't know whether you knew... he had our Primary Sunstone. We have to get a new one. I asked Lallek and Korrek, but they wouldn't help, I think because Shadowmaster Sushin told them not to. So I put my name in for the Achievement of Body. Today. Only somehow... I must have made a mistake... I'm in for the Achievement of Music. But I don't have a composition. The Achievement is in... oh! Ten minutes!"

"Shadowmaster Sushin," muttered Ebbitt. "There are shadows here and no mistake! But first you need some music."

He leaped out of his throne and clambered over a long table, then jumped across to a chest, his Spiritshadow at his heels. From there he crawled under a hammock suspended in a frame. Tal lost sight of him behind a giant silver gong. He reappeared a moment later holding a long scroll.

"'March of the Muldren on Drashamore Hood'!" he exclaimed, weaving and jumping his way back to Tal.

"What?" asked Tal, taking the scroll. It was music, he saw, written in the traditional way, down the scroll. Music on the left side, light on the right.

"Name of the piece," replied Ebbitt. "Never performed. The Muldren were – are – warriors in Aenir, beyond the parts where we Chosen normally go. The Drashamore Hood was a monster, I suppose."

"What happened?" Tal asked, staring down at the scroll.

"Tell you later," Ebbitt said. "You need to get to the Crystal Wood. Within nine minutes."

"Nine," Tal groaned, looking at his Sunstone. "I can't make it."

"We'll have to go by steam. Come on."

Ebbitt took Tal by the arm and led him through the furniture so quickly that Tal knocked several pieces over and banged both knees.

"Steam?" asked Tal. "What do you mean, steam? Where—"

He stopped suddenly as they came to a stairway leading down. A dark stairway. Ebbitt tugged at his arm, but Tal wouldn't move.

"That's going down!" he protested. "I have to go up!"

The maned Spiritshadow nudged him behind his legs and Tal fell forwards, held up only by Ebbitt's surprising strength.

"Have to go down to go up," said Ebbitt, laughing. Tal almost sobbed. His great-uncle had clearly gone completely crazy. He'd given Tal the music, but that was no help. He'd never get to the Crystal Wood now.

They ran through the dark to the bottom of the stairs. They were somewhere in the Underfolk caverns. Tal fumbled at his Sunstone, desperately trying to get some light. He couldn't bear this darkness!

Before Tal could do anything, Ebbitt raised his hand and the Sunstone on his finger blazed into a bright, indigo light – a colour forbidden to Ebbitt since his demotion to the Red.

Tal almost choked as he saw it, and forgot to breathe as Ebbitt moved his hand through a series of gestures, the light following in an almost solid band. Quickly, Ebbitt wove a shining cylinder around himself and Tal.

"Stay very close to me," Ebbitt cautioned. He didn't sound mad any more and Tal knew that the indigo cylinder of light around them was very powerful magic, certainly forbidden to Red Dimmers or Orange boys.

Tal stayed closed to Ebbitt as they shuffled forwards. They came to a large metal door, locked by a wheel. Ebbitt turned it, but didn't open it. He gestured at his Spiritshadow instead. It moved forwards under the cylinder of light and thinned itself, becoming almost invisible. Then it slowly eased itself under the solid metal of the door.

It came back a moment later and nodded. Ebbitt opened the door. A rush of steam came out. Tal flinched, but the steam didn't pass through the blue light. It washed around it and he felt no heat.

Ahead of them, he saw a shaft. Billowing steam

obscured how deep it was and how high up it went.

"Come on," Ebbitt said before stepping forward, seemingly into empty space. Tal hung back, but his great-uncle's grip was too strong.

Tal closed his eyes and followed. Obviously, they were going to fall together, down into the boiling pools of the central heating system.

But they didn't fall. Tal opened his eyes and looked down. Indigo light shimmered under his feet, light solid enough to hold him up and to keep the heat of the steam at bay.

"Stand by for a surge of steam," Ebbitt warned as he closed the door behind him. The light moved out to cover his hands, as if it were cloth. Tal pushed at it experimentally, but it wouldn't budge for him. His shadowguard sat at his feet in the shape of a Dattu, a small, furry rodent that lived in hillsides in Aenir. It was a harmless shape, one the shadowguard took when it didn't like what was happening, but couldn't do anything about it.

"Steam!" shouted Ebbitt and pointed down. Tal looked and saw a solid-looking mass of white surging up the shaft. A moment later, it hit. They were suddenly propelled upwards, so quickly that Tal fell over and even Ebbitt had to kneel and clutch at his Spiritshadow.

Faster and faster they shot up. Tal tried to get up, but some strange force kept him pressed to the floor of indigo light. He felt like several people were lying on him trying to crush him flat.

Then he noticed that Ebbitt was counting, very quickly. At twenty-five, he suddenly pulled at the indigo light in front of him, tugging it away from the wall. Steam instantly rushed through the gap and their rate of ascent slowed.

But they were still going up even faster than Tal had come down the slide. Too fast, it seemed, for Ebbitt. He looked at his Spiritshadow, and it lunged through the light to set its claws in the stone of the shaft.

Instantly, they slowed almost to a stop, accompanied by a hideous screeching sound from the Spiritshadow's claws. Tal started in recognition. He'd heard that sound before, coming from behind the walls. It was always explained as "the heating", but it must have been Ebbitt – or someone – using this strange method of transportation.

"We're there," said Ebbitt. "Or just past it. Three minutes to go. Hang on."

The Spiritshadow let go and they suddenly fell about ten stretches. Steam still swirled around them, but not as much. Tal saw that there was another metal door in front of them. Ebbitt reached out, the indigo light still encasing his hands, and opened it. White light poured in and Tal recognised one of the minor corridors.

From the neutral colour of the Sunstones, he knew he was close to one of the Colourless Corridors, and on the level of the Crystal Wood.

"Out," said Ebbitt. Without warning, his Sunstone flashed and he pushed Tal into the corridor, through the protective barrier of light. The door clanged shut behind the boy. In a second, Great-uncle Ebbitt and his strange steam-driven capsule of light were gone.

Tal got up, checked to make sure he had the scroll, and strode out into the larger corridor. At least now he had a chance – a very slim one, since he didn't know the music and was totally unpractised with the composition.

But it was a chance, Tal told himself. Perhaps his only one...

The Crystal Wood was another of the ancient artefacts of the Castle. It was made up of forty-nine trees of clear crystal, each ten stretches tall and with many branches. The trees stood at the centre of a huge hall, surrounded by tiered benches for the audience.

The magic and marvel of the Crystal Wood lay in the fact that every branch of every tree could produce a single, clear note when it was correctly struck with a beam of light. The duration and intensity of the note depended on the colour of the light beam and how long it touched the branch.

The Wood was played from a central stone, as

tall as a man, with a silver spike set in it that held the scroll.

Tal climbed the stone in a state of eerie calm. He was the first to perform that day and there wasn't much of an audience. He saw a scattering of Chosen from all Orders, save the Violet, who were presumably too important to waste time listening and watching an unproven boy from the Orange.

Tal tried not to look at them as he fastened his scroll to the spike and let it roll down. Fortunately, Ebbitt scribed with a clear, large hand and the symbols were easy to follow. It didn't look too hard a piece to perform.

Tal looked across to where the judges sat. There were three, and they would lead the audience reaction. In theory, everyone was allowed to show the light they wanted, whether it was the Red Ray of Disapproval, the Violet Ray of Attainment or the dreaded White Ray of Disgust. In practice, they would follow the judges, who sat on their own high bench, with clear space to either side, obviously separate from the crowd.

Tal noted that something was going on at the

judges' bench. One judge, a woman of the Green, was smiling and stepping down, making way for someone else. But Tal noted that despite her smile, her Spiritshadow was between her and her replacement, as if there was some danger there.

Tal started to look away, to study the scroll once more, when something about the replacement judge caught his eye. His head whipped back and a terrible feeling surged up in his chest. The replacement judge was Shadowmaster Sushin!

Sushin sat and looked across at Tal. Their eyes met and Tal finally realised that what he saw in the older man's eyes was not merely a look of superiority. It was a look of hatred. Sushin really hated him. But Tal didn't know why. He hadn't done anything!

Shaking, he looked away. He had to concentrate on the Achievement of Music. It didn't matter that Sushin was a judge. If Tal did well enough, he would be rewarded. That was how things worked in the Castle.

All three judges settled at the bench. They looked at one another, then raised their Sunstones to send beams of light rippling at random through the Wood. Light met crystal and music shimmered out through the hall. The audience settled and Tal took a deep breath.

The judges' light beams rippled across again and then withdrew. Tal raised his own Sunstone and said in a voice that was not quite a shout, "I am Tal Graile-Rerem. I will perform a composition of my Great-uncle Ebbitt Nune-Taril, never before seen or heard. It is called 'March of the Muldren on Drashamore Hood'."

As he finished speaking, Tal directed a beam of red light at the outermost branches of the central tree. Maintaining this, he cast out other beams to other trees and branches. Music came from the crystal and light refracted into the air. Both music and light drew a picture. Bold warriors armed themselves on one side of the Wood, while a dark creature heaved itself out of the primordial bog on the other.

Slowly, the two parts of the light and music moved together, building up and up. The warriors circled the monster; the monster made sudden dashes at them. Then, in a crash of light and music that made the audience jump, battle was joined. Colours flashed everywhere as the music leaped and fought, louder and louder, rising to a crescendo.

Then, silence. All colour lost. Four, five seconds passed as the audience held their breath. Who had won? Suddenly, there was a tiny flash of red, the beginning of a tune. Then more red, as the surviving warriors gathered and their song grew louder. Then the joyous sound of triumph. The monster was vanquished; the warriors could return to their homes. They began to march and a column of light swept through the Wood, right to the ends of the branches, and then leaped off seemingly into the audience on a final, long-sustained note.

Tal dropped his Sunstone back into his shirt and bowed. He felt exhausted, but proud. He had made no mistakes. He had performed better than he ever had before and much better than the artists in most of the ordinary Achievements of Music he had seen. Surely he had won his Sunstone!

Then the first Yellow Ray of Failed Ambition hit his face. He looked up and saw that it came from Shadowmaster Sushin. The other judges were looking at him and Tal saw the beginnings of a Violet Ray of Attainment fade. Then they, too, were directing the same light at him. The Ray that was shone for those who tried too hard, who failed to achieve their object. It was not a bad result, as such, for it merely meant that he had tackled something too difficult. He would not be punished or be given deluminents. But he would gain no awards, unless the audience refused to follow the judges.

Tal looked up, hoping his anxiety would not show. There were a few Violet rays coming through, a few Blue Rays of Commendation, an Indigo Ray of Extreme Approval. But not enough. Most of the audience, however reluctantly, was following the judges' lead.

The light in front of Tal grew more and more yellow, till the decision was absolutely clear. Failed Ambition it was. Tal bowed and held up his Sunstone, flashing the Orange of his Order to show his understanding and acceptance.

He climbed down the stone and walked out of the Crystal Wood alone, except for his thoughts. The same thoughts that had been with him for every waking second of the last week.

He had to get a Primary Sunstone. Obviously, he could not hope to win one through an Achievement. There was only one way left to him. Or only one way he could think of.

Tal considered going back to Ebbitt, but that would mean discussing his failed Achievement and he wasn't ready for that now. It always took a lot of energy to talk to Ebbitt, to keep him even partly in the same conversation. Tal didn't have that energy. He couldn't face his mother either. Or Gref and Kusi. They all depended on him, and so far, he was failing.

No. He would go on to his next plan immediately. He would go up to the highest level of the Violet and seek an audience with the Empress.

Tal had never been into the Violet, the highest and most private levels of the Castle, save the Towers.

He was surprised to find that it was really no different than any of the other levels. There seemed to be fewer people around and not all of them were members of the Violet Order. Tal carefully bowed and gave them light anyway, just to be safe. He almost bowed to an Underfolk servant and caught himself just in time.

The only problem was, now that Tal was on the seventh level of the Violet Order, he didn't know where to find the Empress. After wandering around the most obvious corridors, he finally plucked up the courage to ask a Brilliance of the Indigo who didn't seem in too much of a hurry, and whose Spiritshadow was not too frightening. Tal didn't know what it was, but it had four legs, a tail and a head, and wasn't showing lots of teeth. This was a big improvement over some of the horrendous Spiritshadows he'd seen.

"The Empress?" replied the Brilliance. He seemed more amused than annoyed that an Orange boy should ask him such a question. "You seek an audience, I suppose?"

"Yes," said Tal. His shadowguard nodded, too.

The Brilliance laughed. Tal wasn't entirely sure why. Then he gave Tal directions to the Outer Antechamber and to the Imperial Guard. They would decide whether or not to let Tal in.

Tal thanked the Brilliance properly, bowing deeply and giving light. The Brilliance was equally courteous, but he laughed again as Tal walked away.

Without the directions, Tal would never have found the Outer Antechamber. He had to go through several empty rooms and up some more stairs, leading him even higher than the Seventh

Violet. Finally, he came to a much larger room, where several people were lounging about on chairs, drinking and talking.

All their talk stopped as Tal came into the room. Their Spiritshadows leaped up at once and so did two of the Chosen. They were all of the Violet Order, Tal saw, but he didn't recognise the insignia they wore. They each had violet bands on their white robes and wore gold bracers with blazing suns on them, chains of gold filigree and many Sunstones.

Strangely, their Spiritshadows were all the same, which was unusual except in the case of twins or very close siblings. The Spiritshadows were tall, vaguely manlike creatures, but very broad-shouldered and with impossibly thin waists almost like spinning tops. They had no necks and their broad heads seemed to be largely made up of enormous mouths. They also had four arms.

It wasn't until Tal saw that all the Chosen were wearing swords that he realised this must be the Imperial Guard that the Brilliance had told him about. Or some of them, anyway.

Tal bowed and offered light. His shadowguard

sat at his feet, once again assuming the shape of an inoffensive Dattu.

"I am Ethar, Guardian of Her Majesty, Shadowlord of the Violet," said one of the guards, a tall woman who looked about the same age as Tal's mother. "What are you doing here?"

Tal straightened up from his bow, but still kept his eyes down at the floor. Suddenly, he had a feeling that this was not his brightest idea. There was no one else here, apart from the guards. Maybe he should have gone somewhere else. Maybe the Indigo Brilliance had played a trick upon him.

"I… I wanted to see the Empress," Tal stuttered. The deluminents on his wrist jangled as he spoke, reminding him how close he already was to demotion to the Red, or worse. Perhaps he had just earned more deluminents by coming here.

"You want to see the Empress?" Ethar repeated grimly. She strode over to Tal, so she was looking down at him, her Spiritshadow close by, its four arms already stretching out as if it might grab Tal at any moment.

"Yes," said Tal. "I wanted to ask her for a new

Sunstone for my family. We've lost our Primary Sunstone you see, because my father is missing—"

"What is your name?" Ethar interrupted.

"Tal Graile-Rerem," said Tal. "My father, Rerem, is a Shiner of the Fourth Circle. He... he was lost recently on a mission for the Empress."

Out of the corner of his eye Tal saw that Ethar recognised his father's name at least, because she looked back at the other guards for a second.

"So, Tal, why should we let you past to see the Empress?"

"Um, why?" repeated Tal. "Because I need your help?"

All the guards laughed at that and Ethar took a step back, no longer so threatening. Her Spiritshadow slid back, too, decreasing in size until it lay at her feet.

Tal let out a small sigh of relief. Whatever he'd said, they seemed friendlier now.

"It's not as easy as that," Ethar explained. "If you want to see the Empress, you must first ask the Seniors of your own Order and gain passes from them. I don't suppose you've done that?"

"No," said Tal glumly. He thought of Shadowmaster Sushin, Brightstar of the Orange Order. He would make sure Tal never got a pass. "I don't think they'd give me one."

The guards laughed again at that. Tal felt suddenly more angry than scared. Why was it so funny that his family was in trouble and he was doing his best to help them?

"Well, since you're already here," Ethar said, a smile slowly spreading across her face. "I suppose we could play a game. If you win, we'll let you past. If you lose, you can... let me see... give me your Sunstone."

"What game?" whispered Tal. This was a chance, it seemed. But if he lost his Sunstone, he would lose his shadowguard. He would no longer be a Chosen. He would have to join the Underfolk.

Ethar pointed to a side table, between two guards. Tal recognised the tabletop at once, for it was designed to be a game board. There was a row of seven rectangles cut into it around one half of the rim, a round circle of white marble in the middle, and another row of rectangles on the other side. A deck of large, pasteboard cards was on the circle of white marble.

"Beastmaker," said Ethar. "Do you accept the challenge?"

Tal knew how to play Beastmaker, though the sets were rare, since no one knew how to make either the cards or the battlecircle any more. But Great-uncle Ebbitt had a set and Tal had played quite often. Much more often than anyone would suspect of an Orange boy.

"Yes," said Tal, knowing that with one word he had sealed his fate. He would go on to see the Empress, or he would go down to join the Underfolk.

Everything depended on a single game of Beastmaker.

Tal sat down at the game table and Ethar sat opposite. Tal felt strangely calm now that he had accepted the challenge. He looked down at the seven rectangular depressions in the tabletop in front of him. He knew what they were, but he thought he'd pretend to know less about the game. That way Ethar might underestimate him.

"What order are these in again?" he asked, pointing to the rectangles.

"Head, Heart, Temper, Skin, Speed, Strength and Special," said Ethar quickly.

Each rectangle would ultimately hold one card, and that card would specify the characteristics of the beast. The Strength card would determine the beast's strength, the Speed card would determine its quickness, and so on. When all the cards were in place and finalised, two twelve-centimetre-high beasts of solid light would be produced from the combined characteristics, to battle it out in the marble circle in the middle of the table. Whoever played their cards right and produced the victorious beast would win the game.

Each card could be changed twice by using light. So even when a card was in place, and your opponent could see it, it might still change. The trick of the game was to make the other player think you were making a certain sort of beast and then change it at the last moment by altering the cards that governed its seven characteristics.

There was also luck, of course. There were a hundred cards, but each player was only dealt seven, all of which had three possible variations.

Tal hoped that he would be lucky.

Another guard dealt the cards one at a time, as was the usual practice. Tal took his first card and felt the warmth. Beastmaker cards were somehow made with pinhead-sized Sunstones bonded to heavy pasteboard. The Sunstones made them warm, and also created very lifelike pictures of the beasts on the cards. Nearly all of the cards showed creatures from Aenir, plus a few other beasts that didn't seem to exist either in Aenir or the Castle.

Tal's first card was a Phalarope, a marine animal that floated around in the water and had thousands of poisonous tendrils. Its only real use was in the Special category, because then the made beast would have poisonous tendrils. Tal knew that this card would change to a Kurshken if he applied green light from his Sunstone. Kurshken were small but very smart and quick lizards, so would be good in either Speed or Head.

Unfortunately, Tal didn't know what the third variation of the card was. He had a faint memory that it might turn into a Hugthing under red light, but couldn't be sure. Hugthings were particularly nasty. They looked like a carpet of comfortable green moss, but could spring up and wrap themselves around you in an instant. For the game, a Hugthing card would be good in Skin or Strength.

"I will play first, if you like," said Ethar. This would give Tal a slight advantage, so he quickly nodded to say yes.

"Heart of a Borzog," announced Ethar, laying the card down on the second rectangle in front of her. Tal looked at the card, which showed a fearsome, semi-human and very hairy creature roughly the size of three people across the shoulders. This was a good initial play. Borzogs would fight to the death and beyond. Once they got a grip, they never let go, even when they were killed. Strong-hearted indeed.

"Um, err, Head of a... whatever this is..." announced Tal, playing the Phalarope into the Head rectangle. He was going to change it into a Kurshken later on, but he hoped Ethar would think he didn't know what he was doing.

"A Phalarope," said Ethar. She looked at the bulbous thing with its many tentacles and added, "It does look something like a giant brain."

"That's what I thought," said Tal, pretending he was relieved. "A giant brain. Perfect for the Head."

The other guard dealt them both another card. Tal picked his up slowly. At first, all he could see was a pair of red eyes in the card. Then he slowly became aware of an outline around them. The card was showing him something hidden in a cave or a hole, with only the eyes visible.

Then Tal remembered and barely suppressed a shiver of horror. This card was of a Cavernmouth. They were horrible creatures in Aenir, who dug holes for themselves in the side of a mountain and then backed in and opened their enormous jaws. What he thought were glowing eyes were actually something like tonsils at the back of the thing's throat.

Whenever anything came close enough, the Cavernmouth's extendable jaws would snap out, grab its prey and drag it inside to be slowly digested.

In the game of Beastmaker, the Cavernmouth card was unusual. It could be played in Speed, because its jaws were incredibly fast at snapping out. Or it could be played in Special, to give the created beast extendable jaws.

The variations were not so useful, or at least not as far as Tal knew. Orange light would turn the card into a Jorbit, which was a fairly fast, dim-witted, nocturnal grass-eater. Violet light would change it to a Rorarch, one of the strange stone creatures of Aenir. This would seem useful in Skin, but actually the Rorarch was very brittle stone and could be broken into little pieces by a single, sharp blow. Tal didn't want the beast he made to shatter at the first hit, and he wasn't sure where else the Rorarch could be played.

"Speed of a Gorblag," said Ethar, playing a card that looked like a large, glowing blue toad that was too fat to do anything. But one of the variations of the Gorblag card was the incredibly zappy Fleamite, an insect that could move faster than a human eye could track it. Tal knew Ethar would change that card later on.

"Speed of a Cavernmouth," Tal countered, playing his card. He wouldn't be changing that. Even if Ethar did change her Speed card to the Fleamite, it wouldn't be much faster than a Cavernmouth.

"You have played before," remarked Ethar. "Few people remember the Cavernmouth can be played for Speed."

"I saw my great-uncle use it that way once," Tal

said, still trying to give the impression he was an absolute beginner at Beastmaker.

The game moved more swiftly then. Within a few minutes both Tal and Ethar had six of their seven rectangles filled with cards. If they filled the seventh, their beast would be made, without a chance to change any of the existing cards. Ethar had left her Strength rectangle empty and Tal, the Temper.

As Tal had expected, Ethar started to change her cards instead of playing her seventh. With each change, Tal became more concerned. He was changing his, too, but he wasn't sure he was going to end up with the better beast.

"You hid your skill well," said Ethar as she changed the mild-mannered Klatha workbeast in her Temper rectangle to the insanely vicious Vengenarl, a creature that attacked even its own kind if they trespassed over its scent-marked boundaries.

Tal nodded, but he wasn't paying attention to what Ethar said. Everything depended on him getting the best beast. Now that Ethar had changed the Temper of her beast, Tal thought he knew what to play there. But once he put that card down, his beast would be complete. Did he need to make any changes?

Quickly, he scanned the seven rectangles. Head of a Kurshken. Skin of a Samheal Semidragon. Temper... that was to come. Heart of a Hrugen, which was a gamble, since that was actually a kind of weed that never gave up; it grew everywhere in Aenir and seemingly could not be eradicated. Speed of a Cavernmouth. Strength of a Jarghoul, a cannibalistic strangling snake of the jungles of Aenir that primarily ate others of its own kind after weeks-long battles to crush one another to death; Special, the ability of the Gossamer Bug to fly.

Tal ran over all the variations in his head, while Ethar arched her fingers into a steeple and waited for his move.

"To see the Empress or lose your Sunstone," she said. "What is it to be?"

"Temper of an Icefang," said Tal, playing his final card, locking all the others in. This was his greatest gamble. He didn't know enough about this card or its properties. But he remembered Great-uncle Ebbitt saying that the Icefangs of Aenir were among the most dangerous of creatures in the spirit world. They never got angry, or demoralised, or had any emotions at all, it seemed. They just coldly fought to the very best of their ability, never distracted by danger, wounds or anything else.

"And Strength of a... Jarghoul," said Ethar, playing exactly the same card as Tal. "Let the battle begin!"

Both Tal and Ethar stepped back from the table as the final cards were played. Although no one knew how to make Beastmaker boards any more, everyone had heard about the one that exploded years before, every Sunstone in it suddenly igniting.

But this Beastmaker board seemed to work perfectly. The cards in their rectangles began to slowly glow brighter and brighter and a luminous mist formed on each side of the table. Then the two clouds of mist drifted across to the battlecircle in the middle of the table and began to form into shapes.

Tal held his breath, wondering what his beast would look like. Inside his head, he urged the formless lump of bright mist on, willing it to be the best beast ever made, a champion that would win his entry to see the Empress. Soon, all his troubles could be over!

Then his cloud of bright mist solidified into a brightly coloured beast. It was tall and slender and had the general shape of a lizard, except it stood up on its hind legs and had wings. Its skin was scaly and iridescent, sparkling in many different colours. Its huge, delicate-looking wings were also multi-coloured and almost translucent.

It was pretty. It was even beautiful. But didn't look at all tough or dangerous.

Tal let out his breath in disappointment and shut his eyes. He didn't want to look at the opposing beast, which had also solidified out of the glowing ball of mist on the other side of the circle.

"Interesting," said Ethar in a puzzled tone. Tal opened one eye a fraction. Ethar's beast was really ugly. It resembled a blubbery, rust-coloured ball that had three arm-legs coming out of the top and three out of the bottom. It had four pairs of eyes spaced around its middle, and a separate, many-toothed mouth under each pair of eyes.

As Tal watched, it flipped over on to its top legs and then flipped back again, very quickly. Then it deliberately fell back and actually bounced high into the air, without using its arm-legs at all.

Tal's beast just watched the bouncy ball thing and stood there, its wings flickering like a hummingbird's. It was only when Tal looked closely that he realised it wasn't standing – it was hovering a couple of centimetres above the white marble of the battlecircle.

The battlecircle began to change colour from white marble to red, the sign that the combat would commence. Tal took a step closer, as did Ethar and all the guards, who crowded around.

Quickly, Tal looked over at Ethar's cards hoping he would see some flaw that his beast would exploit.

Ethar had played the Head of a Dofyn, which was fairly standard play, since the Dofyns were the enormously clever sea dwellers of Aenir. Then the Heart of a Niphrain Ape. The Temper of a Vengenarl. The Skin of a Blorem, which as far as

Tal could remember would give the beast a skin of very resilient, thick blubber. The Speed of a Fleamite. The Strength of a Jarghoul. And finally, the Special of an Urglegurgle. Tal had no idea what that was, but now that he'd seen the made beast, he figured it had to be bouncing.

The battlecircle flashed red three times. On the third flash, Tal's lizard suddenly shot forwards, just as Ethar's blubber-tub bounced. They met in a whirring of wings, teeth and clawed arms – or legs – and parted just as quickly.

"By the Light!! A hit!" cried Ethar, pointing to the drops of bright emerald-green blood that were welling out of the lizard-beast's forearms.

"Mine, too," said Tal, pointing at some ugly gashes in the blubber of the bouncing beast. But his heart sank, for the blubber was very thick and the gashes did not look deep.

Before Tal had finished speaking, the blubber-tub attacked again, acting on its Vengenarl temper. This time, the lizard-beast didn't meet it, but flew to one side, zipping and darting around in the air as the blubber-tub bounced and lunged, reaching out its multiple arm-legs to grab and rend.

The lizard-beast was too quick to be caught, but the blubber-tub was also too quick for it to easily strike. They bounced and flew, feinting attacks and withdrawals, moving so swiftly it was almost impossible to follow.

Then the lizard-thing suddenly swooped in and bit out the blubber-tub's eye. It shrieked in rage, the first sound either beast had made, and one of its three-fingered limbs gripped the very edge of the lizard-beast's wing.

There was a tearing sound and part of the wing came off. The lizard-beast leaped back, but clearly it could no longer fly.

"No!" Tal groaned.

The lizard-beast made a yipping sound to taunt the blubber-tub on, as if it didn't care about its torn wing. The blubber-tub, its eye socket bleeding, threw itself back and then bounced forwards to crush its opponent.

But even without wings, the lizard-beast was very fast. It zipped sideways and a claw struck in to take out another of the blubber-tub's eyes. Furious, the great ball of blubber changed direction to hurl itself at the rainbow-coloured lizard.

Once again, the lizard-beast got out of the way just in time. Then it suddenly moved back, as the blubber-tub was changing direction, and bit the bulbous creature on the foot.

"Yes!" shouted Tal, punching the air. The lizard had bitten clean through the blubber-tub's leg, severing the foot.

It still had two on that side, though, and one of the other legs swung across, smacking the lizard in the head. The brightly coloured beast was thrown halfway across the circle by the blow and seemed to be stunned. It lay there, unmoving, while the blubber-tub did a flip to get back on the three good legs on its other side.

"Get up! Go, lizard!" yelled Tal.

"Kill it!" shouted Ethar. The other guards shouted, too, some encouraging Tal's beast, some encouraging Ethar's.

Slowly and murderously, the blubber-tub advanced on the motionless lizard. Then it started to bounce. A small bounce, then a slightly harder one, until it was bounding up a quarter stretch or more. With each bounce, it got closer and closer to the defenceless lizard. It clearly intended to crush Tal's beast to death.

Tal looked on, horrified. Even though the creatures were only created things of magical light, he couldn't bear to see his lizard killed. He stopped thinking about everything that depended on this little beast of many colours. He just wanted it to survive.

As the blubber-tub shot up for what had to be its final bounce, Tal shut his eyes. He felt sick. Everything was over now.

Suddenly, the guards roared, but it was a shout of surprise, not triumph, from Ethar. Tal's eyes flashed open and saw the lizard-beast flying around a stunned blubber-tub, darting in to pluck out its eyes one by one.

"What happened?" he asked one of the guards who had been betting on his lizard.

"It tricked the blubber-thing," said the guard happily. "That lizard's got four or five layers of wing. It could still fly and it wasn't knocked out. Smart beast, kid."

But despite losing more of its eyes the battle was not yet over for the blubber-tub. It had the Heart of a Niphrain Ape, so it could not give up. Bleeding from a dozen wounds, it lurched after the lizard, chasing it around and around the battlecircle.

"Only a matter of time now, boy," said the friendly guard. "Well—"

Whatever the guard was going to say stopped in his throat, as the far door suddenly swung open with the screech of disused hinges. Like everyone else, Tal looked over.

Something huge and very, very dark was coming through the door. A Spiritshadow, Tal realised, but one bigger than he'd ever seen. Its head was all spikes and flanges, as wide and tall as the door, so it struggled to get through. A sinuous neck followed, but whatever body lay behind was too big, unless the Spiritshadow chose to shrink it.

Suddenly, Tal realised he was the only one still standing up. All the guards had fallen to their knees and were bowing in the Spiritshadow's direction. Tal stood there gawping, till his shadowguard reached up and pulled him down by the front of his tunic.

Only then did he realise what... or who... this Spiritshadow was. It had to be Sharrakor the Mighty, the Empress's own Spiritshadow. The Shadowdragon that alone among its kind had a name.

Sharrakor's vast head reared up on its serpentine neck and its jaws opened. Tal saw teeth of shadow and swirling patterns of darkness.

Then Sharrakor spat a great glob of shadow that fizzed through the air, straight at Tal!

Tal ducked, but the shadowspit wasn't aimed at him anyway. It struck the Beastmaker table. There was a flash of light, a sudden sizzling noise, and the still battling lizard-beast and blubber-tub were gone.

Tal looked at the empty battlecircle, where small shadows ran like water over the side of the table and on to the floor. He cringed as several shadow patches flowed past him, back towards Sharrakor. Tal realised, shivering, that the Spiritshadow had spat some portion of itself. Now all those small shadows were rejoining the whole.

Tal cleared his throat, about to protest the Spiritshadow's destruction of the game, but his shadowguard leaped up and thrust itself into his mouth, an instant gag. Tal reached up to pull it free, but the friendly Imperial Guard gripped him as well so he couldn't move.

The last pieces of shadowspit rejoined Sharrakor. The Shadowdragon's head swung heavily from side to side, as if seeking another target. Then it slowly withdrew back the way it had come. When it had fully withdrawn, the door creaked shut behind it.

Tal's shadowguard dropped out of his mouth and the Imperial Guards visibly relaxed.

"What—" Tal began to say, but he got no further. The friendly guard and Ethar picked him up and practically threw him out of the other door.

"Go!" said the friendly guard. "Go!"

"But I won!" Tal protested. "At least my beast was winning!"

"We should not have played," said Ethar, frowning. "It was my mistake, so you shall not be punished further."

"But I—" said Tal.

"Sharrakor came because the Empress did not like an Orange boy in the Upper Violet," said Ethar roughly. She pushed Tal quite hard in the chest, sending him staggering back, his shadowguard trying to hold him up around the legs. "Go back down, boy!"

Tal stared at her for a moment, furious at being cheated. But what he saw in Ethar's eyes was not anger or loathing, but fear. The friendly guard was afraid, too.

"I'll be back," muttered Tal. "I'll see the Empress! I'll get my Sunstone!"

Then his courage failed him, for whatever scared two Shining Ones of the Violet was more than enough to scare Tal. He turned round and ran, back down the stairs to the normal Violet levels, then in a rush to the laundry chute.

Tal rode the chute all the way down forty-eight levels, from Seventh Violet to First Red. The leather soles of his shoes were smoking when he finally stopped.

He had come so close to winning the game of Beastmaker, to being let through to see the Empress.

But, Tal thought miserably, he hadn't won. He hadn't got a new Sunstone. All his plans had come to nothing and he had no new ideas. He thought of his mother, sleeping the sleep of sickness in her sunchamber. Of Gref trying to escape the blinding lights of Lectorium bullies. Of Kusi, who was too young to understand, but still cried because she knew everyone else was upset. And of his father, lost somewhere in the dark, trusting that Tal was looking after the family.

Great-uncle Ebbitt was his last hope. Surely Ebbitt would think of something.

The wardrobe of white bone was gone, though it had been there only that morning. It seemed such a long time ago because so much had happened. Not for the first time, Tal wondered how Ebbitt moved everything around so quickly.

Tal moved cautiously through the furniture. He wasn't in the mood for one of Ebbitt's practical jokes, particularly since they often involved some sort of mild injury.

But his great-uncle was clearly in sight when Tal rounded a marble statue of a Chosen, caught forever in the stance of a light-sculptor, Sunstone at the ready. That was a good sign. When Ebbitt hid, the practical jokes were always much worse.

Coincidentally, the old man was sitting by a Beastmaker table, idly shuffling the cards. He got up as Tal approached.

"How was the Achievement?" he asked. "I heard it was a superb performance."

"I got the Yellow Ray of Failed Ambition," said Tal sullenly.

"I didn't ask about your results," snapped Ebbitt. "You would never be properly rewarded with Sushin as one of the judges."

"But why?" Tal sat down in a convenient, but too large chair and rested his head in his hands. "Everything I do, there seems to be someone against me!"

"Probably because there is," Ebbitt observed. "Sushin for one. He's always hated your father for besting him in the Achievement of Combat. Eight times, I believe, over the years. But he wouldn't dare act alone. I'm afraid that someone higher up has taken a dislike to our family."

"Who?" asked Tal.

"I don't know," said Ebbitt. Without warning, he suddenly pursed his lips and whistled a complicated birdcall, then cocked his head as if expecting a reply. When none came, he continued. "But I'll find out. Now, where have you been? The Achievement finished hours ago."

"I went to see the Empress—"

"You what?!" exclaimed Ebbitt.

"But the guards wouldn't let me in," Tal continued. "Ethar said she would if I won a game of Beastmaker, and I was winning, but then Sharrakor—"

"Sharrakor!" exclaimed Ebbitt, gripping his white hair and doing a strange, frenzied dance across to Tal.

"Sharrakor came in and spat on the game and the beasts disappeared," said Tal. "Then Ethar and another guard kicked me out."

"Thank the Sun and the Stars and all things of Light," said Ebbitt, sinking to his knees. "Don't you know anything, boy? You must never, ever go to the Empress without permission!"

"I just wanted to get a Sunstone," Tal said wearily. It seemed he couldn't do anything right. "I have to get a Sunstone somehow. I've asked the cousins and tried to win an Achievement and tried to see the Empress. I can't think of anything else."

"Why not?" said Ebbitt. "You are my grand-nephew, aren't you? You must have inherited some of my tremendous thinking power."

"I don't know," said Tal. He wasn't sure Ebbitt had all that great thinking power. He had lots of weird thought power, but that wasn't the same.

"Where can you find Sunstones?" asked Ebbitt. "Sunstones that no one owns yet. Lots and lots of lovely Sunstones, ripe for the taking."

"Nowhere," Tal replied glumly.

Ebbitt stretched out his hands towards the ceiling and capered around in a circle, singing, "Up in the Sun, the Glorious Sun, where Stone Fingers stretch and stretch, up through the darksome Veil!"

"You mean the Towers?" asked Tal, unable to believe what Ebbitt was suggesting.

"Yes," said Ebbitt. He stopped capering and kneeled down next to Tal, suddenly serious. "It's dangerous, but I believe it is the only hope now. All the usual means of gaining a Sunstone will be blocked by Sushin or the Chosen he is in league with. You will have to climb one of the towers and steal a Sunstone. Steal several while you're at it."

"Steal a Sunstone?" asked Tal. "But what about the guards, and the Spiritshadows, and the traps?"

"Try the Red Tower," said Ebbitt. "It will be the least protected. Your shadowguard looks pretty smart. It'll help you find the traps."

Tal looked at his shadowguard. It had taken a shape similar to Tal's natural shadow, but with the chest bravely puffed out. Obviously, it thought stealing a Sunstone was a good idea.

"How would I start?" asked Tal. "I don't even know how to get outside."

"I know," said Ebbitt. "Underfolk ways, unseen by Chosen. I'll show you."

Tal stared at the old man and then down at his puffed-up shadowguard. It sounded extremely risky, but he really couldn't think of anything else.

"All right," he said finally. "But first I want to go home and have a rest."

And, he thought, he could say goodbye to his mother, and Gref, and Kusi.

In case he didn't come back.

"Excellent!" exclaimed Ebbitt. "I'm sure you'll have lots of fun!"

PART 2:
AFTER

"Lots of fun, lots of fun, lots of fun, lots of fun... "

Ebbitt's voice was echoing inside Tal's head, accompanied by a weird, really loud rushing noise. It was also incredibly cold and dark. For a few seconds, Tal thought that he was in the middle of an awful nightmare. Any moment now he would wake up to the soft light of his sleeping chamber...

But he was awake!

He had taken Ebbitt's advice. He had climbed the Red Tower. And he'd fallen off, right through the Veil. In just a few seconds, he would hit the Castle roofs and that would—

Suddenly, Tal realised that he wasn't falling

down so much as sideways, like a feather blown on the wind. Something was also gripping him quite painfully around the chest and waist.

Tal craned his head around, but couldn't see. It was absolutely black, the darkest he had ever experienced. Dark so fearful that his hand automatically went to his Sunstone.

But it wasn't there. The chain was still around his neck, but the Sunstone itself seemed to have gone. Desperately, Tal pulled at the chain, hoping that his fingers would find the Sunstone.

But the chain was caught somehow. It wouldn't move. Tal tugged at it again and light suddenly blossomed behind him. At the same time, there was a sound that Tal found unbelievably comforting – his shadowguard's warning hiss!

He craned his head back again and saw that his shadowguard was gripping him. It had made four arms to hold him tight and a pair of very long, very thin wings. That was why he wasn't falling! He and the shadowguard were gliding on the wind.

Tal laughed, a crazy laugh of relief. He was speeding away from the Castle, carried by the wind, out into darkness. But he had his shadowguard and he had his Sunstone – he hoped.

The laughter stopped as everything went black again. Tal clutched at his chain. It was still there. He tugged on it and the shadowguard hissed. Tal tugged again and the shadowguard hissed louder.

Finally, Tal understood. The shadowguard must have formed around the Sunstone, drawing every little bit of the stone's light to make itself as big and strong as it could. All shadows needed light to exist. Without the Sunstone, the shadowguard would dissipate in this total darkness under the Veil.

There was a lot of snow. Cold, wet lumps kept hitting Tal in the face. He had become totally soaked by them. He remembered blacking out, but not for how long. By the feel of his frozen hands and face, it had been for quite a long time.

He looked down. There was nothing to see but darkness, a dark so terrifying that Tal had to shut his eyes. It was better to pretend to be asleep than to look into a world without light.

In fact, Tal thought, maybe he was dead. This was what happened after life. There wasn't anything outside the Castle. He'd died and gone somewhere else. Perhaps he would fall forever...

But he didn't feel like he was dead. He could feel his body, which was shivering with both cold and fear. He felt the shadowguard shift a little, try to flow around him to give him extra protection from the wind, but most of its shadowflesh was being used in the wings that kept them gliding.

On and on they flew. Tal lost track of time and all feeling in his face and hands. He opened his eyes every now and then, blinking against the onrush of snow and ice, blinking away his own frozen tears. But there was still no sign of light.

Later, Tal was almost unconscious again and totally frozen. He thought he was going to die and that this horrible flight through darkness and snow would never end. Then he saw it. A bright glow somewhere ahead and below.

"The Castle!" Tal shouted, or tried to, but his lips were frozen together, and all that came out was a muffled cry.

The shadowguard tilted its wings and they turned towards the distant light. Surely it was the

Castle, Tal thought, not caring that the wind must have taken them away from his home. As far as he knew, there was nothing else in the whole Dark World. It had to be the Castle.

But as they flew closer, he became puzzled, his tired, frozen mind grappling with what he saw. The light was too small to be coming from the Castle, too feeble. There should be hundreds of lights, thousands of lights!

He was still wondering what it might be when the shadowguard suddenly hissed and flapped its wings in a frenzy, desperately trying to slow them down.

Three very long seconds later, Tal and his winged shadowguard ploughed into the side of a hill, snow spraying out in all directions as they bored into a deep, wet drift.

12

They went a long way into the drift. So far that Tal seriously thought he'd be smothered before he could claw his way back to the surface. At least the shadowguard had let go of his Sunstone, so he had some light and could tell which way was up.

Or so he thought. Being buried in the drift was a bit like being underwater. The cold, wet snow was all around him and kept getting in his mouth and nose every time he tried to breathe. The only way to move was to use a half-swimming, half-digging action.

Fortunately, the Sunstone warmed him and lit his path. When Tal finally clambered out of the drift and staggered to a point where he was only up to his waist in snow, he held the Sunstone up and concentrated on it. It grew brighter and waves of warm air flowed from it over Tal's hands and sopping wet clothes.

Tal groaned and grimaced as the warm air returned feeling to his frozen hands and face.

Tal stood there for what seemed like hours with the warm air flowing around him, as much as he could generate from the Sunstone. But he still couldn't get really warm. His shadowguard was draped across his shoulders like an extra cloak, but it didn't help.

Even worse than the cold was his sense of disorientation. There was nothing but snow around him, as far as his Sunstone's light fell. There were no other lights in the darkness.

It was a completely alien landscape, even stranger to Tal than the spirit world of Aenir. At least he had been there before and was trained to cope with it. He also knew how to leave Aenir. What if he was trapped in this cold wasteland forever?

The warmth of his Sunstone helped Tal think a

little. It was familiar and comforting, even if did melt the snow around his legs and make them wetter as the rest of him got dry.

"I have to get back to the Castle," said Tal. Saying it aloud made it seem more likely that he would. On his shoulder, the shadowguard made itself a head and nodded in agreement.

Saying it was easier than doing it, Tal thought as he looked around. The Sunstone illuminated a small area around him, but even ten stretches away it was dark again. There was no sign of that other light he'd seen from above.

"Which way is the Castle?" he asked, hoping his shadowguard would know.

It shuffled on his shoulder and then extruded a thin, one-fingered arm that pointed off at a right angle.

"That way," said Tal. It looked the same as any other way. "How far?"

The shadowguard did not answer, but he felt it make a motion like a shrug. Tal thought about the question for a moment, then rephrased it. He was used to working at communication with the shadowguard. He often had to ask the same question several different ways.

"How far to the Castle in stretches?" asked Tal. Distances inside the Castle were measured in stretches. Tal knew his arm from shoulder to wrist was almost exactly one stretch. They didn't need a larger measure.

The shadowguard extended a hand and grew ten or twelve fingers, which it wiggled up and down too quickly to count.

"A long way," Tal translated. He knew it had to be, but he'd somehow hoped it wasn't. "Well, I guess I'd better start walking."

Following the direction the shadowguard had given, he started to push through the snow. It was hard work, harder than he expected. The snow was tightly packed and though the envelope of warm air around him melted it a little, it was not enough to make walking easier.

After a few hundred stretches of this, Tal was exhausted. He'd started to sneeze, too, and could feel fluid spreading in his chest, making it harder to breathe. Back in the Castle, he would simply have gone to his parents, who could heal such simple ailments with their Sunstones. But Tal had not yet learned Healing and so could only suffer.

But he wouldn't give up. Far away, his mother lay ill in her bed. And what had happened to Gref? What if the Spiritshadow that had taken Gref was like the one that had attacked Tal above the Veil? Gref could be dead or lying wounded somewhere. Tal had to get back as soon as he could.

After a while, the snow got shallower, and while it was easier to walk through, Tal started to slip more often. He realised he was walking on ice, under a light dusting of snow.

"One, two, three… "

He started counting steps. Somewhere around a thousand he lost track of what he was up to and had to start again. His shadowguard was also having to point out the right direction every few minutes, as Tal started to turn into a circle. Everything looked the same. Ice and more ice, with nothing to see.

He was up to one thousand and ninety-eight steps when he suddenly realised that while he was still counting aloud, his legs had stopped moving.

In fact, he had fallen over in the snow, too weary to immediately realise what was going on.

The shadowguard was tugging at him, hissing, trying to lever him back up again. Tal laughed at its efforts, a hysterical laugh that surprised him because what was happening was the exact opposite of funny. But he did get up, and staggered on a few steps, his laughter turning into a choking cough.

Then he saw the light. A strange, soft green light that was moving over the ice faster than he could run. For a moment he thought it was two enormous green eyes in the head of a huge monster, sprinting towards him.

Then, as it drew closer and slowed, he saw that the light was coming from a box that was being drawn across the ice, in harness, by six shaggy-haired, four-legged creatures with tall heads and spiky branches sticking out between what he presumed were ears.

The box was some sort of cart, Tal realised, like the ones the Underfolk used to move things around. But it had very long, thin sort of feet-things, Tal guessed, instead of wheels.

The soft green light came from the globes that were mounted on either side of the strange cart. They were made of tightly woven strips of bone, with the light coming through the gaps in the weave.

Then Tal noticed that there was someone in the contraption. For a second he felt incredible relief. It had to be some of the Underfolk. He'd never really understood where they got all the food and goods used by the Chosen. Obviously, they came out here to get something. He would commandeer their strange transport and have them take him back to the Castle immediately.

"Thank the Light," he gasped, staggering forwards, holding up his Sunstone, ready to show light and prove himself a Chosen.

The next thing he knew, he was face down on the ice, with his shadowguard wrapped round his knees – just as a spear whistled through the air exactly where his head had been!

Tal's attacker made a horrible keening noise as Tal desperately rolled to the side. New energy came from pure fright, as he pushed himself up and tried to run away.

But the spear-thrower was in front of him. A short monster covered in furs, concealing everything of its form. Its face was totally white, as pale as bone, with hideous markings and deep-set yellow eyes. Its mouth was a round, dark hole.

It also had an axe, a great-bladed thing, not of metal, but some sort of carved bone or translucent stone.

Instinctively, Tal raised his Sunstone and

directed a blast of white-hot light at the creature. It yowled like a cat, raised one arm to shield itself and advanced on its hind legs, swinging the axe viciously from side to side.

Tal stumbled back, while trying to keep the light focused on the creature's eyes. But it had tucked its chin into its chest, avoiding the beam. Even like this, it still came on, howling and chopping with its axe, the blade cutting the air just in front of Tal as he retreated.

It would catch him soon. He was too tired to keep focusing on his Sunstone and would slip. If he didn't do something else, he would be chopped into bits.

The shadowguard realised that, too, and Tal felt it slip off his shoulders. It fell to the ground as a dark splotch, but was up again immediately, as a Corvile that dashed at Tal's attacker.

The creature, head down, didn't see it until it was too late. The shadowguard nipped at one knee, shadow-teeth ripping through fur and possibly the flesh underneath.

"Ow!" exclaimed the monster, sounding

surprisingly human. "By the Crone, you'll pay for that!"

Tal almost stopped in surprise as he heard that voice. This wasn't a monster. It was a girl! The hideous face was a mask, with amber lenses in the eyeholes!

Girl or monster, she was still very dangerous. She saw Tal's surprise and lunged forwards, the blunt end of her axe striking him in the stomach with a sickening thud. Winded, Tal crumpled to the ice, his light beam shooting off into the sky.

"No, no," he begged, holding up one hand as if he could ward off the axe blow that followed. "Don't kill me!"

"Die, thief!" she shouted in return. "This is Far-Raider's Ice!"

Everything seemed to happen in slow motion then. Tal saw the girl raise her axe high above her head, the blade glinting in the Sunstone's light. The shadowguard was wrapped around her leg, biting, but she paid it no attention.

Higher and higher the axe went and Tal could hear the deep indrawing of the girl's breath as she prepared for a blow that would cut him in half.

Then, even as the axe came swinging down, someone else shouted. The loud, commanding voice of a woman who was used to being obeyed.

"Milla! Stop!"

But the call came too late to stop the axe. Tal stared at it, mesmerised, the moment of its fall drawn out into what seemed like a whole lifetime of terror.

In the very last fragment of a second, Milla's wrists twitched and the axe smashed into the ground by Tal's head, smashing chips of ice all over his face.

He lay there, stunned, as the girl slid back her mask to reveal a pale, oval-shaped face and striking green eyes. But there was a spark there of extreme anger, and her cheeks were flushed with emotion.

"Don't think you'll live, shadow-eater," she growled, bending down so her face was close to Tal's, so close he could feel the heat coming off her skin. "The Crone will deliver you to me. We will fight again."

Then she stalked off, out of Tal's sight. His shadowguard came slinking back, to wrap round his neck. It seemed to be quite pleased to get away from this mad girl, too.

Tal kept lying still. It seemed to be the best thing to do, to gather his strength. He still had his Sunstone, and could use that better now that he was not surprised. He could see that the girl had only a natural shadow. She wasn't a Chosen, which meant that he had been right in guessing the Underfolk came out here, or once did. This girl did not look anything like any Underfolk he had ever seen. Her face was pale but red-cheeked, her hair white-blonde and her eyes piercingly green. Tal had never seen hair that colour, and he realised he had never seen an Underfolk's eyes. They always kept their faces lowered.

He was still lying there when whoever had called out came to look down at him. This was an older woman, her mask already off. She had different clothing, though, softer-looking furs. Tal realised Milla had some sort of armour on as well, but this woman didn't. She didn't have an axe either.

"Get up," said the woman. "Or I'll have Milla cut you into pieces and feed you to the Wreska."

Tal got up. As his shadowguard moved, the woman stepped back, sucking air between her teeth.

"What is that?" she asked.

Tal thought for a moment, unsure of how to respond. These people, with their natural shadows, had to be some sort of Underfolk. There was only one way to treat Underfolk and that was to give them orders. Possibly they still hadn't realised he was a Chosen!

"My shadowguard," said Tal proudly. "I am Tal Graile-Rerem, of the Orange Order of the Chosen of the Castle. Who are you?"

This seemed to be the wrong thing to say. Milla, who had been walking away, suddenly turned with a growl and hefted her axe. But the older woman raised her hand and the warrior girl stopped.

"He does not know our ways," said the woman. "A strange thing to find upon the ice. There is much here that we should know."

She paused, thinking, then said, "I am the Crone of the Far-Raider Clan of the Icecarls. That is Milla, who wishes to be a Shield Maiden, and may yet be. You will come with us back to the ship, Tal Graile-Rerem."

She pronounced his name strangely and Tal didn't like the way she spoke to him at all. She only had a native shadow, after all.

"You will take me to the Castle," he commanded. "At once."

His voice quavered and it sounded weak even to him. The business about showing Underfolk who was the boss clearly didn't work here. These Underfolk were feral. They might do anything.

"Um, please," he added, his voice breaking completely.

The Crone looked at him, then turned towards Milla. Tal didn't see what she did, but Milla pulled something out from under her furs. A flat, curved bone that she held by one end.

Tal was still wondering what it was when it hit him in the head and knocked him unconscious.

As Tal fell, his shadowguard caught him and lowered him down. Before it could do anything else, the Crone sprang on it, holding open the mouth of a large bag. She scooped up lots of snow, but also scooped up the shadowguard.

The shadowguard started to ooze through the

tough Selski skin of the bag, but again the Crone was ready. She tucked Tal's Sunstone into his shirt, hiding its light.

"Without light, the shadow that walks alone cannot prosper," she announced in the darkness. "This is known to the Crones, Milla. I shall follow your sleigh, not too close, for fear the light will awaken it."

"Do I have to take that?" asked Milla petulantly, pointing at Tal.

"Yes," said the Crone. "And be quick. He is only a boy and he has the wet sickness in his lungs. We must get him to the ship before a death sets upon him."

"I shall set his death," whispered Milla. She grunted as she picked up his arms and started to drag him back to her sleigh. "If he'd been a normal raider, I would be wearing my first winner-sign by sleeptime!"

"But he is not a raider of any kind, normal or not," said the Crone. Her eyes seemed to shine in the darkness, though the lights on the sleigh were too far away for any reflection. "Quickly, child! Do I have to tell you everything twice?!"

Tal slowly regained consciousness. His hearing came back first, his ears filled with strange sounds. There was a faint humming all around and a crunching sound that welled up through his bones.

He opened his eyes and they swam into focus. It wasn't dark, for which he was very thankful. Good Sunstone light fell on his face, bright and warm. But there was other light, too, around the edges. Soft, green light.

Tal's head hurt. So did just about every other part of him. He was warm, though, thanks to the furs that someone had put on him while he was unconscious. It felt strange to have so much weight on him, but given the temperature, it was welcome.

He sat up, coughed, and looked around.

He was on the deck of a vessel of some kind, a very large one, with three masts, well over a hundred stretches long and twenty wide. This was obviously the ship the Crone had talked about. Tal knew about boats and ships from Aenir, but this ship was sailing across the ice. Tal had no idea how it managed to slide so easily.

The sails above him were full, moving the ship along faster than Tal would have been able to run. The humming came from the wind in the rigging. The crunching, cutting sound came from a vibration that he could feel right through the deck, something to do with the way the ship moved.

Tal guessed that it was like Milla's weird cart-thing drawn by the – what were they? – Wreska. This ship was driven by the wind, but it must be supported on similar long, thin rails that cut into the ice.

There were people moving around on the deck. More Underfolk, with normal shadows. They all wore furs and skins and most had vicious-looking weapons. None of them seemed at all interested in Tal.

He stared at them. They were like Beastmaker cards come to life or illustrations from a story. Tal was tempted to touch one to see if that really was hair all the way down to his waist. The lump on his head told him that would not be a good idea.

The familiar light came from what had to be a large Sunstone, somewhere up above. Tal squinted and saw that it was somehow attached to the very top of the tallest mast, the middle one. A powerful Sunstone indeed, or perhaps a cluster of stones, for it illuminated not only all the ship, but the ice for several hundred stretches around.

But for all its power, there was something wrong with the Sunstone, Tal saw. The light flickered, instead of being true and strong, and the colour changed a little every time the ship rocked or hit a bump.

The green light came from more of the tightly woven globes that Tal had seen before. One was quite close, so he got up and looked at it. As he'd thought, it was made of thin strips of something like bone, woven so there were tiny holes in the weave. Something buzzed around inside and created the green light.

"Moths," said a voice behind him. "Luminous moths."

Tal turned around. It was the old woman, the one who'd called herself the Crone. She was holding a pottery urn. Tal's eyes were instantly drawn to it and he felt a wave of dizziness. For a second, it felt like he was inside the urn, unable to get out. At the same moment, he realised that his shadowguard was nowhere to be seen. Both things made him feel like throwing up.

"Your shadow is trapped in here," said the Crone, noticing Tal's frantic glances all around him. "It shall be released, if we decide to let you live."

"You wouldn't dare kill me," exclaimed Tal hotly. "You're Underfolk! The Chosen and their Spiritshadows will... will kill everyone on this ship if you do!"

The Crone didn't say anything, but she kept looking at him. Her eyes were luminous, Tal realised, bright with some internal light that was not reflected. He felt them boring into him, as if the Crone could read his mind.

After a minute, Tal looked away and said, "I suppose they wouldn't, actually. They don't even know where I am. None of us ever leave the Castle anyway."

"But *you* have," said the Crone. "Tell me of this Castle, and why you have come here, to the hunting grounds of the Far-Raiders."

Tal wiped his nose with his sleeve. He was still having difficulty coping with the fact that these people – who he *hoped* were Underfolk – could decide whether he lived or died. But there didn't seem to be any choice.

"Here," said the Crone. She set the urn down, close to Tal and pulled a small wooden bottle out of her furs. Tal took it suspiciously, but drank. As the liquid went down his throat, he felt it spread warmth.

Slowly, occasionally sipping from the bottle, Tal began to talk. The Crone interrupted him from time to time, asking questions, but mostly she just let him talk. Tal was surprised to find himself saying so much. He even told the Crone about his father's disappearance, and his mother being sick, and how worried he was about what might have happened to Gref, which was probably his fault, too.

By the time he finished, a whole crowd of Icecarls was listening. Most of them were pretending to be doing something else, like coiling rope or looking overboard. Some just stood, or sat, and listened. They did not seem hostile.

Except for Milla, who Tal realised had been above him, up the mast, all along. Listening and watching, ready to drop on him if he attacked the Crone.

"A fine story there," said one of the Icecarls, a huge man with a beard dyed blue and plaited into three strands. "Do you have any others, boy?"

Tal stared at him. Clearly, the man thought he'd made it all up.

"It's true," he protested. "I am one of the Chosen. I come from the Castle."

The Icecarl chuckled and said, "You'd not be the first boy who lost his ship and went storytelling around the Clans. But if you're not a storyteller, you must be a thief on our hunting grounds."

A murmur went around the crowd of Icecarls at the word *thief*. Tal felt a new hostility directed at him. Whatever these people did to thieves, it couldn't be good.

"If he is a thief, Forkbeard," the Crone said, "you can give him to the ice and the Merwin will take him."

"I'm not a thief!" exclaimed Tal. "And I am telling the truth. I'll prove it to you!"

He pointed up to the flickering Sunstone, past Milla's scowling face. She spat downwind, a clear indication of her opinion of Tal's truthfulness.

"Your Sunstone must once have given a clear, steady light," he said. "Now it flickers and changes colour."

"Any fool knows that!" said Forkbeard. He looked angry now and was stroking his axe. "Any fool who's seen a Sunstone, though there's few enough around the Clans. Give him to the ice, I say!"

"But I can fix it," stammered Tal. "It just needs tuning."

"Good," said the Crone. "I was hoping you would say that. If you can mend our Sunstone, we will spare your life."

"If he can't mend it, can I fight him?" asked Milla. She dropped down from the mast, landing lightly on her feet. Tal instinctively moved back, closer to the urn with his shadowguard in it.

"No," said the Crone, her voice stern. "If he fails, he goes to the ice – and the Merwin."

Tal had expected the Icecarls to bring the Sunstone down to him. But the Crone explained that they only did that when the ship was anchored. They needed the Sunstone's light to see any dangers that might lie ahead.

When Tal refused to climb, Milla took special delight in describing exactly what a Merwin was, and Tal's chances of surviving a meeting with one.

"Most Merwin are about ten times as long as you are tall," she said. "They have a single, shining horn that sticks out the front between their eyes. See Kral over there? That sword of his is a baby Merwin's horn. They stop glowing once they're dead. Now the Merwin slide over the ice faster than you'd be able to run because their skin is so slick and they've got four big flippers to push themselves along. Mostly they stick their horn through whatever they're after, and then they bash it up and down on the ice. You'd be better off fighting me. All you have to do is ask. If you ask to fight me, the Crone will let you."

Tal ignored her. He didn't understand why she was so keen to fight him, but he knew that the Crone would protect him… as long as he fixed the Sunstone.

"I'll need my shadowguard," he said. "I need it to help me climb and fix the Sunstone."

The Crone looked at him again with those creepy, glowing eyes. Then she said, "No you don't."

Tal sighed. He didn't really, absolutely need his shadowguard, but he felt very strange without it nearby, dizzy and sick to his stomach. Climbing the mast would be ten times as hard without the shadowguard, even if it just followed him like a normal shadow.

"Milla will help you climb up," said the Crone.

"I will not!" exclaimed Milla. "He's a lying thief!

You cannot believe his talk of hundreds of lights and this 'castle' thing—"

The Crone turned her gaze to the girl and said, "You wish to be a Shield Maiden, Milla, but you won't follow orders?"

The threat was clear. Tal didn't know what a Shield Maiden was, but Milla obviously really wanted to be one and the Crone had the power to stop her.

Milla turned to Tal with a murderous scowl on her face and said, "All right! Start climbing, thief!"

"My name is Tal Graile-Rerem," Tal said. "I shall permit you to call me Tal. And even if I was a thief, you don't have anything I'd want to steal!"

At least, he told himself, he wasn't a thief as far as the Icecarls were concerned.

"Tal, Smal, Bal, Wal – whatever you call yourself," Milla said. "I don't suppose you can climb a line, so we'll have to go up the mast itself."

She pointed at the spikes that were stuck into the mast every stretch or so. Tal went over and put his foot on one, testing its strength. Then he reached up and started to climb.

The mast appeared to be a single bone of some kind, though Tal couldn't imagine what kind of monster would have a backbone forty stretches long. And the handholds weren't spikes as he'd thought. They were smaller bones that had been sawn off. Once they would have been like the bones of a fish, curving out from the backbone.

"Hurry up," called Milla from below.

Tal ignored her. The mast was swaying, and the ship and the ice seemed a long way down. For some weird reason it was scarier than when he climbed the Red Tower, though that was hundreds of times as high. Perhaps it was because there was no shadowguard to save him.

Milla kept harassing him all the way to the top, calling out and trying to crowd him. Tal focused his mind on climbing and ignored her.

Finally, Tal came to the Sunstone. It was held to the top of the mast by what seemed like large, curved teeth that were somehow bonded to the bone. The stone was so bright Tal had difficulty looking at it without his shadowguard to automatically shield his eyes.

Milla fell silent as they approached the stone. She also stopped several stretches below instead of crowding Tal as she'd done all the way up. Her head was bowed. Clearly, she couldn't stand the brightness of the Sunstone, not this close.

This high up the mast, Tal had the strange illusion that he was still and it was the ship and the ice below that swung from side to side like a pendulum. Each time the world swung by, Tal had to fight back the feeling that he was going to fly off into space.

To make it even worse, he had to let go of one of his handholds to touch the Sunstone. It was a powerful stone, but Tal knew it was also very old. Sunstones did wear out eventually and had to be taken up to a Tower to be revitalised above the Veil.

Making sure he had a good grip with his left hand, Tal reached out and touched the Sunstone. He could feel the currents of power within it. Just as he learned in the Lectorium, Tal closed his eyes and focused his thoughts upon the Sunstone.

As he'd thought, it badly needed tuning. What power it had left was working against itself, rather than together. The energy bands needed to be realigned, brought back into harmony.

Tal carefully let go of the big Sunstone and reached into his shirt to pull his own Sunstone out. It brightened as he focused upon it, to find the correct pattern of energies and project it at the Icecarls' Sunstone.

It was hard work with the wind all around, the mast swaying and his stomach suddenly deciding it didn't like the Crone's warming cordial after all. But Tal did it. A beam of pure light shot out of his Sunstone and into the Icecarls' larger stone.

"I've done it!" exclaimed Tal triumphantly. The Icecarls' stone shone bright and true.

Then it went out, and so did Tal's own stone, leaving him in total darkness, save the faint green glow of the moth-lamps on the deck far below.

The roar of anger that came up from the deck was almost animal in its intensity. Tal had never heard anything like it. He glanced down, but couldn't see anything, not even Milla. Still, he could hear what was happening.

Every Icecarl aboard was leaping on to the ropes and rigging, climbing up to kill the boy who had ruined their Sunstone, their greatest treasure.

Tal's only hope was to get it going again. Unfortunately, he didn't even know why it had gone out.

Desperately, he grabbed his own Sunstone, no longer caring if he fell off. He focused on it, feeling for its power. It felt like his whole body and mind were bent on this one thing, every particle of his power concentrated on one small stone.

The power was still there, Tal perceived. But it had somehow retreated into the depths of the stone. He had to bring it out, open it up, before Milla threw him off the mast. As he thought that, Tal felt her hand grip his ankle. Her fingers tightened, ready to pull him away.

"Light begets light," Tal heard his father's voice say, echoing up from the depths of his memory. That was one of the first lessons learned by every Chosen. Tal had heard it on his father's knee, when he was no older than Kusi was now.

Light begets light.

But he had no light. Milla was prying his foot away from the mast. He had to create some light to restart the Sunstones. He had to do something!

One foot came free and Milla gave a shout of triumph. Tal kicked at her, but that made his position even worse. He slipped down a rung and the chain around his neck broke. He still held the Sunstone, but that left only one hand for the mast.

"Quick as a Sunstone spark," said another voice in his mind. Great-uncle Ebbitt's voice. "Quick as a Sunstone spark."

"Light!" screamed Tal. Balancing solely on one foot he struck the two Sunstones together. A huge spark shot out as they met and all of a sudden his Sunstone burst back into glorious light. A moment later, so did the Icecarls' stone. It was brighter than it had been before and the colour was even, without flickering.

Milla put the foot she held back on to a rung and silently began to climb back down.

Tal looked and saw Icecarls everywhere, dropping back down on to the deck. He swallowed and took several very slow breaths.

"Thank you, Father," he whispered to the wind. "Thank you, Great-uncle Ebbitt."

Then he slowly climbed down, too. It had been a narrow escape.

On the deck, the Crone was waiting. Forkbeard stood next to her, his axe in its sheath upon his back.

"You have done as you said," she said. "So we will do likewise. We will not give you to the ice."

Tal nodded. Then, without knowing why he bothered to tell her more, he said, "I've only mended it for a while. The Sunstone is old. It will fade in time and there is nothing I can do to make it last longer."

"Yes," said the Crone. "It is known that Sunstones die, as do all things upon the ice. But you have helped us now."

"And you have shown that I accused you falsely!" said Forkbeard. He raised his voice and added, "I, Grim Forkbeard, say it so all can hear. You spoke truly, Tal. To mend my wrong, I... I offer to adopt you as my son and take you into the Clan of the Far-Raiders, blood and bone."

Tal stared at him. Obviously, these people weren't really Underfolk, so the offer wasn't a complete insult.

But I don't want to be adopted; I have to get back home!

He started to answer, then saw the Crone narrow her eyes at him, as if in unspoken warning.

That made him think and pause. Among these savages, Grim Forkbeard seemed quite important.

He was also extremely large and fierce-looking. It was best to be polite to him, even if he wasn't one of the Chosen.

"I thank you, Grim Forkbeard," he said, bowing and raising his Sunstone, though he only let it spark out a little light. "But I have my own family in the Castle and I must return there as soon as I can."

Forkbeard nodded. He looked a bit relieved, as if he'd been forced to make his offer out of good manners. Tal was surprised, because he wouldn't have thought the Icecarls had anything like manners.

The Crone nodded, too.

"Wisely spoken, Tal," she said. "Let us go below. We will eat Selski meat, drink vitska and talk of what your future holds. Milla, you will come, too."

The Crone picked up the urn with Tal's shadowguard and led the way to an open hatch.

Tal was surprised to see that below decks was a large, open space. All the Icecarls lived together down here. Light was provided by tall tubes of some clear material, filled with water and floating clots of jelly that shone with a yellowish light. As Tal passed by one of these tubes, he tapped it. The clots of jelly rushed to his finger and he saw that they were marine creatures.

"Glowjellies," said the Crone. "Hard to catch, under the Ice."

She led the way between sleeping Icecarls who were just lying against the curved ribs of the ship, wrapped in their furs. Tal was careful not to step on any of them, for all lay with their weapons by their hands and he saw that many opened one eye as he approached.

As Tal's eyes adjusted more to the dim light, he saw that while it was a large, open space, there were partitions here and there. But even these only had thick curtains instead of doors. Curtains of fur and shiny black hide.

The Crone led Tal to one of these curtains and pulled it back, revealing a small chamber. A low table was in the middle, surrounded by cushions of all shapes and sizes.

"Sit," said the Crone as she placed the urn down. Tal sat down next to it and touched the smooth side, as if he might feel his shadowguard through the fired clay.

Milla sat down, too, as far away as she could. The Crone went back out, leaving the two of them alone.

For a while, Tal tried to meet Milla's stare, but after she went for several minutes without blinking he got tired of that and looked away. She laughed, a scornful laugh that made him mad. But there was nothing he could do. She wanted him to attack her with his Sunstone, Tal knew.

She wanted an excuse to fight him.

Before Milla or Tal cracked and started to fight, the Crone came back in, carrying a bowl of something that steamed and smelled rather disgusting. She put it on the table and gave Tal an object that he supposed was meant to be a fork, though it was made of bone and only had two tines.

"Selski meat," the Crone said. "The lifeblood of our people. Where the Selski go, we follow, taking their old, the ill and the weak. Selski meat fills our stomachs, Selski skin gives us clothes and sails, Selski bone our tools and weapons, Selski gut the strings for our harps."

"It tastes better than it smells," she added,

pushing the bowl towards Tal. She must have seen his nose wrinkle.

Reluctantly, Tal jabbed at a piece of the meat and put it in his mouth. Suddenly, as he tasted it, he became ravenous. It did taste all right, but mostly he was just incredibly hungry.

The Crone left while he ate, but Milla sat there, staring. If she blinked, she did it while Tal wasn't looking. She didn't eat either.

"Why don't you have some?" Tal asked when he had eaten his fill. He pushed the bowl towards her tentatively, almost like a peace offering.

"A Shield Maiden does not eat in front of a prisoner," Milla said stiffly. "A Shield Maiden does not sleep in front of a prisoner. A Shield Maiden—"

"Tal is not a prisoner," interrupted the Crone, who had come back in. She held the curtain back to let whoever was with her in.

It was a very old woman, Tal saw. A hunched over, wrinkled and faded lady, who was not much bigger than Gref. She looked at Tal and he saw that her eyes were milky, without pupils. She was clearly blind.

The effect she had on Milla was striking. The girl leaped to her feet and pushed her clenched fists together in salute.

"Mother Crone!" Milla exclaimed.

Tal got up, too, since it seemed to be the thing to do. From Milla's exclamation, he figured that this blind old lady was more important than the Crone.

"This is the Mother Crone, most ancient and wise," said the Crone, leading the old lady over to Tal. "She has come to see what your future holds and help us decide what must be done with you."

The old lady did not speak. She took Tal's hands in her own and turned the palms up. Then with one long, very yellow fingernail, she traced the lines from his wrist across the palm.

Tal let her do it, but only because Milla was there and he knew she would do something to him if he tore his hand away. It felt really weird having this ancient fingernail drag across his skin. He couldn't help staring at it, so long and yellow, more like the talon of an animal than a human fingernail.

Then the Mother Crone lifted his hand to her face and pressed his fingers against her milky eyes. Tal flinched and his disgust must have shown on his face, for Milla took a step forwards, anger in her eyes.

Anything might have happened then, but the Mother Crone spoke, and at the sound of her voice, everyone was still. It wasn't loud, but it seemed to echo inside Tal's head. Even when the voice got softer, Tal found that he could hear nothing else. All the background noises of ship, ice and Icecarls faded away.

There was only the voice of the Mother Crone.

Far have you fallen
Yet not so far

> *Long must you travel*
> *Yet not so long*

Home is the Castle
Yet it is not home

> *Shadows befriend you*
> *Yet are not friends*

Shield Maiden stands by you
Yet not back to back

Light warms you
Yet shadows fall

Blood binds you
Yet binds you not

Evil hunts you
Yet hungers not

Darkness hides you
Yet blinds you not

Sunstones fall from you
Yet into others' hands.

The voice trailed away. Tal sat down suddenly, the echo still going on inside his head. He was hardly aware of saying goodbye to the Mother Crone as she was led past the curtain, into waiting hands.

"That seems clear," said the Crone. She smiled,

for the first time that Tal had seen, showing very white teeth.

"What seems clear?" Tal muttered. He felt really woozy, like he'd just woken up from a very long sleep.

"We're going to help you get back to your Castle. And you are going to get us a new Sunstone."

That broke Tal out of his dreamy state. "What?!"

"The Mother Crone has prophesied," said the Crone. "We will send someone with you, to help you on the ice. When you get back to the Castle, you will give her a Sunstone in return."

"Her?" asked Tal suspiciously.

"Milla," replied the Crone, smiling again. "It will be her Shield Maiden Quest to see you safely to the Mountain of Light and to your Castle that is built upon it."

"What!" screamed Milla. "How could you do this to me?"

"'A Shield Maiden faces her faults,'" recited the Crone, still smiling. "Besides, this is the greatest Quest I have ever given – to go to the Mountain of Light, to bring back a Sunstone."

"So you knew where the Castle was all along?" interrupted Tal. "You knew I was telling the truth?"

"Yes," said the Crone. "The Crones know of it, for your Castle is the only permanently bright thing in the sky, there atop its mountain. But it is forbidden to us, for we know it houses great evil, where shadows rule."

"That's not true!" exclaimed Tal. "Shadowspirits serve us. The Chosen rule them. They are servants, like my shadowguard you keep locked up there. That's all."

"That is no more than a Selski sprat is to a Merwin," said the Crone. She wasn't smiling now. "We know of what these shadows are, how our ancestors fought them and raised the darkness that protects us."

"Your ancestors!" said Tal. "They had nothing to do with the Veil. The Chosen made it because the sun is too strong."

"Don't speak to the Crone like that," said Milla and she raised her fist.

"Enough!" said the Crone. "We must bind you to the Quest. Tal, give me your arm."

Slowly, Tal put out his arm. The Crone took it and slid the sleeve of his fur coat back, to show his bare wrist. Tal waited, thinking she was going to read the future in it or say something like the Mother Crone had said. He was totally unprepared when she suddenly produced a large tusk and sliced it across his skin.

"Ahhh!" he shouted, pulling his hand back. Blood was already welling out. Tal saw that the Crone had actually cut him three times, very swiftly, making a strange, triangular pattern in his skin.

"Weakling," commented Milla and she held out her wrist. It was already scarred in the triangular pattern. The Crone cut near the old scars and Milla watched the blood appear without flinching.

"Clench your fist to keep the blood coming," instructed the Crone. "And follow me."

"Keep it flowing?" asked Tal. These Icecarls were even madder than he thought. But he did clench his fist, watching the beads of blood come out. The Crone hadn't cut deep at all. She must have had lots of practice. Tal shuddered, thinking what might have happened if she wasn't so good at it.

They went back on to the deck. The Sunstone on the mast was still shining brightly, which Tal was glad to see. But it was snowing again, heavily, and visibility was poor. He kept his head tucked in as the Crone led him to the mast.

There she took his wrist and wiped the blood against the mast and then the deck. From the different colour of the bone there, Tal guessed this ceremony had been done many times before. Milla did the same.

"Repeat these words after me," said the Crone, once more looking into Tal's eyes with her strange, luminous gaze. He nodded, licked his lips and ate a snowflake by accident.

"I give my blood to the bone, bone of the ship," said the Crone.

"I give my blood to the bone, bone of the ship," repeated Tal and Milla. The Crone took his wrist and wiped it on the mast and the deck again. Milla followed.

"I give my blood to the Clan, Clan of my blood," said the Crone.

"I give my blood to the Clan, Clan of my blood," repeated Tal. The Crone took his wrist and forced it against Milla's upturned wrist, so their blood mingled. Milla looked away.

"I give my blood to the wind, blood to the ice," said the Crone, taking Tal's hand and shaking it so a drop of blood was taken by the wind and carried overboard.

Milla shook hers at the same time and, by some freak of the wind, the drops of blood met. But only the Crone's eyes were sharp enough to see that happen.

"By bone of the ship and blood of the Clan, I will gain a Sunstone for the Clan of the Far-Raiders. May wind destroy me and ice freeze me if I fail," said the Crone.

Both Tal and Milla repeated the words, with the Crone holding their wrists.

"Now you are bound together in this Quest," the Crone said with satisfaction. "And Tal, you are at least a little bit an Icecarl."

Milla muttered something that was lost in the wind. Tal looked at her and didn't see any sudden friendliness. They might be bound together for a Quest, but he still didn't trust her and she obviously still hated him.

"Milla, show Tal where he can sleep and then prepare for your journey. The Castle lies beyond the Selski migration and there is a gap ahead. You will have to cross it quickly."

"By sleigh?" asked Milla stiffly. "Surely the boy cannot skate or ski."

"You may have a sleigh and six Wreska," said the Crone. "Jorntil will ready them for you."

"Hold on," said Tal. "You mean it's just the two of us who are going? I thought the ship—"

"No," said the Crone. "We follow the Selski, who only know one path. That is our life and we cannot break it except at direst need. Milla will safeguard you. She is an expert hunter, one of the best on the ice. Your greatest danger will be time, for the Selski teem in uncountable numbers. We call it the Living Sea and the gaps in their migration path are narrow. But I am sure you will get across."

She turned away before Tal could ask another question, leaving him standing there, next to Milla. She was looking at her wrist. Tal looked at his and saw that the blood had already dried. The pattern remained.

"Follow me," said Milla, and she crossed the snow-slippery deck and went back through the hatch. Tal followed more clumsily. The Crone had said to sleep, but he didn't know how he was going to do that.

At the hatch, he looked back up at the Sunstone, half-shrouded in the flurries of snow.

He gripped his own Sunstone and thought about exactly how much trouble he was in.

He was incredibly far away from the Castle. In just two months, he had to have a new Primary Sunstone or else he could never be a proper Chosen, his whole future, the whole rest of his life lost. His mother – he choked a little as he thought of her lying ill on her bed – needed that Sunstone. So did Gref and Kusi. His father, if he was still alive, would be counting on him to look after everyone else.

He had just sworn some sort of oath that he didn't mean to keep, but couldn't help taking seriously. He'd mingled his blood with – he didn't know what any more because they weren't Underfolk – but a crazy girl with a natural shadow who wanted to kill him and was only stopped by tradition.

When he woke up in the morning, he would have to leave even the small comforts of the ship and head out across the ice with the crazy girl, to cross a living sea of animals.

It was all too much. Tal gulped and fought back the tears that were forming in his eyes. It's just the wind, he told himself, but he knew that wasn't true.

Then he saw the Crone again. She was standing near the mast. She looked at him and threw something. Tal ducked, but whatever it was hit the deck and then rolled towards him. Something dark, which he instinctively reached for.

His shadowguard flowed past his feet, taking on his form, just like a natural shadow, and spread down the steps behind him. Tal had to look over his shoulder to see it as he sighed with relief.

"I have spoken to it," said the Crone, her voice carrying across the deck. "No one should be without their shadow. But as long as you travel with Icecarls, it must only be a shadow. There is no place for uncertainty about such things on the ice."

Tal smiled and went below. His shadow preceded him, looking no different from any Icecarl's. Tal had no idea if the Crone had taken away its power to change shape and make itself more solid. He didn't care. He was too tired to think about it now. He was just glad to have it back.

"I will wake you at the turn of the glowjellies," said Milla, as she showed him a pile of furs between two snoring boys about his own age. She hesitated, then said in quite a matter-of-fact tone, "I still wish to kill you, but I see that I cannot. Not now we are bound to the Quest. I will protect you on the ice and we will reach your Castle and gain the Sunstone."

Two Sunstones, Tal thought tiredly. He burrowed down in his furs. Everything had begun because he'd just wanted one Sunstone. What was going to happen now that he needed two?

Beside him, his shadowguard suddenly turned into a tiny version of Sharrakor, the Shadowdragon. Milla saw it flicker out of the corner of her eye and whirled around.

But by then it had become a normal shadow again and Tal was sound asleep.

Milla woke Tal up what seemed like only an hour or two later, though his Sunstone said seven hours had passed. She didn't say anything, but just dumped a pile of heavy furs on his stomach, which hurt.

Obviously, the furs were meant for him to wear. His Sunstone could be used to keep him warm, but after it had gone dark the night before, Tal didn't want to draw any power from it unless he had to.

The furs came in three distinct sets. Tal had to experiment with them for a while before he worked out that the light, waist-length one with hanging ribbons went on first, then the leggings, which tied to the ribbons, then the knee-length coat that went over everything. Even after trying it a few different ways, Tal wasn't entirely sure that the outer coat wasn't on backwards. Not that the Icecarls seemed to care very much about how their clothes were worn.

They were very scruffy compared to the Chosen, Tal thought. He was only wearing the furs because he didn't have a full-strength Sunstone.

Milla came back while Tal was struggling with the thick Selski-skin gauntlets. She sniffed and helped him tie them on to his sleeves, so they would be ready to wear and could not be dropped or lost.

"We must be prepared to leave as soon as the Afterguard report a break in the Living Sea," the Icecarl girl said coldly. "Come on."

Tal followed her, his shadowguard dutifully remaining behind him like a normal shadow. It had even expanded to match his increased size. He felt weird under all the fur. It was like suddenly becoming very fat, for he was at least half a stretch wider than he used to be.

Even so, the broad Selski-skin belt he wore seemed to have been made for someone twice that size again. It kept slipping down, though he'd drawn it through the bone buckle as tightly as he could. Obviously, it was Milla's idea of a joke. She didn't want him to be comfortable.

The ship was strangely still when Tal climbed out into the bright light of the Sunstone high above on the mast. At first, he couldn't work out why, as he narrowed his eyes against the light. Then he saw that the ship wasn't moving. The sails were furled, and huge anchor ropes led over the stern and off into the darkness of the ice.

The wind still howled through the rigging and cut at Tal's face. He pulled out the bone face mask Milla had given him and slipped it on. It didn't fit properly, with one eyehole too far to one side to see through clearly. Tal fiddled around with it for a while before giving up and slipping on his gauntlets. His fingernails were already turning blue.

Milla went to the side and easily climbed over, disappearing from view. Tal followed clumsily, hitching at his belt. He hoped she hadn't just jumped down to the ice, because the deck was at least eight stretches high. She might be able to jump down that far, but he knew he couldn't.

She hadn't jumped. There was a ladder, another backbone of some kind, this time made with quite long side-bones or ribs. Tal climbed down after her, much more slowly than he normally would.

There were quite a few Icecarls already on the ice. Eight were returning from a hunting expedition, dragging a huge cube of bloody meat behind them. It was enormous and Tal couldn't imagine what it had been carved out of. A Selski, perhaps.

Another Icecarl was holding the reins of the lead Wreska in a string of six, harnessed to the cart-thing Tal now knew was called a sleigh. The Icecarl had to be Jorntil, who the Crone had said would prepare the animals for them. As they approached, he touched his clenched fist to the hand that held the reins, in a fairly casual salute.

Milla responded by clapping her clenched fists together hard enough to make Tal wince. He raised his Sunstone and let out a small light, and it was Jorntil's turn to wince and look away.

"Sorry," said Tal quickly. "I was trying to be—"

"Get in the sleigh!" hissed Milla. But Jorntil only blinked, laughed and fed the lead Wreska something that looked like the Selski meat Tal had eaten aboard the ship. That made Tal realise he hadn't eaten breakfast, or whatever these strange people ate when they woke up.

Tal didn't want to ask Milla about it and give her another chance to show off that she was tougher than he was. Instead, he climbed aboard the sleigh. It rocked as he pulled himself up and Tal was surprised by how lightly constructed it was. Most of it was made of very thin bones woven together and the whole contraption creaked as he shifted his weight. It didn't seem strong enough to carry him, let alone the two of them.

To make matters worse, the part Tal was standing in didn't seem all that well connected to the two long, bladelike skates underneath. It was like a baby's bouncing basket, Tal thought, peering down. The two skates were solidly joined at the front and rear. The woven bone box he was in was precariously balanced between these supports, held up by six or seven wide bands of Selski skin. These springs would absorb the shock of hitting small bumps and holes, at the cost of bouncing around.

There were two spears and a whip in a long scabbard on the outside of the sleigh. For a moment, Tal thought about grabbing one and throwing it at Milla, and had a daydream about making his escape. But he couldn't drive the Wreska and even with the shadowguard to point the way, he knew nothing about crossing the Living Sea.

The triple cut on his wrist burned as he thought of this, but Tal hardly noticed. There were enough good reasons to put up with Milla for the moment. Later, he would find a way to get rid of her.

Milla jumped in and the whole thing bounced even more. Tal, unprepared, fell against her and she pushed him off.

"Hang on," she said scornfully. She pulled a long whip out of the scabbard on the outside of the sleigh and with a practised flick cracked it out to one side, sending ice crystals flying. The Wreska stirred in their traces and blew out of their noses, sending jets of powdery snow all around.

Milla cracked the whip to one side again and then, in a fluid movement, sent it out over the lead Wreska's head. As it cracked, the Wreska snorted even louder and the sleigh gave a sudden lurch.

"Eeeyyy-aarrr-haaaah!" screamed Milla, nearly deafening Tal. The Wreska responded by lurching forwards, their shaggy legs and sharp three-toed hooves driving against the ice. The sleigh rocked and picked up speed.

"This is fun!" said Tal, startled by how quickly the sleigh was moving. They were moving across the ice faster than he could run, almost as fast as he slid down the laundry shaft back in the Castle.

"It is not fun," scowled Milla. "It is only a means of travel. We are on a serious Quest. There is no time for fun."

Tal didn't answer. Despite what Milla said, riding in the sleigh was fun. But the most important thing was that he was heading back to the Castle. He had been diverted from his own quest, but it wasn't over. He would get a Sunstone and become a full-fledged Chosen. He would do it for his father, mother, Gref and Kusi.

20

All too soon, the sleigh left the circle of light cast by the Icecarls' great Sunstone. Once again, Tal felt the fear of darkness and his hand crept to the newly mended chain around his neck. But there were two of the pale green moth-lamps on the sleigh and the Wreska's antlers, as the spiky branches on their heads were called, also glowed with faint luminescence.

Milla noticed Tal reach for his Sunstone and he saw her smile. Slowly, he forced himself to let go of the chain. He didn't want to let her know he was afraid.

They drove on in silence for an hour or more and Tal soon found that Milla was at least partly right.

He found the speed of the sleigh exciting at first, but after a while, standing up as it bounced and swayed over the lumpy ice made his knees sore and his fingers were aching from holding on to the side.

Not being able to see properly where they were going also made him nervous, though Milla did not seem concerned. Either she could see a lot better than he could in the dim light of the lanterns, or the Wreska could, and she trusted them.

After another hour, Tal was nearly fainting from weariness. He had slumped down, no longer trying to match Milla's upright stance. His shadowguard was the only thing propping him up, though it didn't dare do too much, since it had been told to behave like a natural shadow in order to placate the Icecarls.

"Will we stop soon?" Tal asked finally, when his weariness overcame his pride.

"Yes," said Milla. "We have nearly come to the Living Sea, by my reckoning. We should see the Selski – yes, there is the glow."

She pointed, at the same time hauling back on the reins to slow the Wreska down. Tal looked where she indicated. At first, he couldn't see anything, but as they drew closer, he saw that the ice slanted gently down in front of them. Off in the distance and a little below them, there was a dull glow that seemed to cover all the horizon ahead.

"What is that light?" he asked.

"Kalakoi," said Milla, making a circle with her thumb and forefinger. "They are small... things... about so big, that grow on the Selski. They glow and bring moths and the Slepenish that the Selski eat. But the Kalakoi also eat the Selski, when they grow old and do not scrape enough of them off."

"Um, what are the Slurpernesh?" It grated on Tal that as a Chosen he had to ask these questions of a natural, but it was important to know.

"Sleep-en-ish," corrected Milla. "They go in front of the Selski always. They swarm in uncountable numbers, more even than the Selski. The Slepenish come up through the ice, and if the Selski do not eat them, they go back through it into the water below. Some say that these survivors change into something else in the deep water and birth new Slepenish. I do not know if this is true."

"What do they look like?" asked Tal nervously. He didn't like the sound of things that bored through the ice in uncountable numbers.

"Like the string of a harp, but you never see just one," said Milla. She seemed to struggle with her desire to treat Tal like dirt and an equal desire to show off her knowledge. Showing off won.

"They roil together, more in a single paced square than snowflakes in a storm. They are not dangerous, but when they first come through the ice they weaken it. That is why we never cross between the different hordes of the Living Sea, but only in the temporary gaps. There is always open water where Selski and Slepenish first meet."

Tal was silent for a while, digesting this information. The sleigh continued more slowly, heading down the slope in the ice. The glow grew brighter. Tal watched it nervously, understanding more about what the Icecarls meant when they called the Selski migration path the Living Sea. Certainly, the light of their passage seemed to fill all the world ahead.

Suddenly, Milla pulled hard on the reins and

called out the names of the two leaders, "Tarah! Rall!"

The Wreska came to a sliding, ice-shard-scattering halt. Milla pulled a spear out of the scabbard, choosing the one with the largest head, a wickedly pointed piece of bone as wide and long as Tal's arm.

"What is it?" asked Tal as he pulled out his Sunstone and raised it. All he could see was the glow in the distance. But as the Wreska stopped snorting, he heard a dull rumble as well, a sound like many distant drums. Low, loud and continuous.

"Rogue Selski," snapped Milla. She jumped down on to the ice and lifted her face mask to see better. "Broken off from the horde. We have to push it back in."

Tal peered into the distance. There was something there, dark upon the ice. He'd taken it for a small hillock or mound of some kind. Now he realised it was moving. Heading towards them.

"That's a Selski?" he asked in amazement. It had to be a hundred stretches long and twenty high. It was almost as big as the Icecarls' ship, a great hulking black mass covered in glowing spots that made a pattern like the star-filled night above the Veil.

It was lifting itself up on its huge forelegs – or foreflippers – and then leaping and sliding forwards. It was close enough now for Tal to hear the ice crack and shatter every time it came down. The sleigh shivered under his feet.

"Can't we just leave it alone?"

"No," said Milla. "Rogues are a danger to the ship and other Clans. It must be turned back to the horde."

"You won't be able to do anything to it with that." Tal nodded at her spear. The girl was even madder than he thought. Nothing could possibly turn that huge monster!

"A full harpoon would be better," Milla agreed, in the same sort of tone a Chosen performer might use to describe an Achievement that was not quite worthy of the Indigo Ray of Extreme Approval. She drew her knife – another sharpened, curved bone – and added, "I will have to climb up between leaps and blind it in the left eye. That will make it turn aside."

"No!" Tal exclaimed. He couldn't get back to the Castle without Milla. She might be a dangerous lunatic, but he couldn't afford to lose her, at least not yet. "What about our Quest? That has to be more important, doesn't it?"

Milla hesitated. For the first time, Tal saw her as a girl his own age. She looked like his friends at the Lectorium when they were asked a question they couldn't answer. Then the familiar control came back and her face settled into its stern pattern.

"You are... correct," said Milla with obvious reluctance. She returned knife and spear to their scabbards, lowered her face mask and jumped back on the sleigh. "The Quest is of the first importance. The Foreguard will take care of the rogue."

Tal breathed a sigh of relief and slipped his Sunstone back under his furs. Milla whipped the Wreska up again and the sleigh moved off, turning a little to pass behind the rogue Selski.

"You do not need to be afraid," Milla said as they came closer. She had seen Tal shiver as ice chips blew across them from the Selski's strange leaping progress. "The Selski never turn back. They will change direction to one side, but never back."

A bit like an Icecarl, Tal thought. He peered at Milla through the amber eyepieces of his mask. She was obviously very brave. Climbing that Selski would have meant her own death for certain, but Tal knew she would have done it if he hadn't given her a good reason not to. He was reluctant to admit it, but he couldn't think of many Chosen who would die for their Order. Of course, they lived in a much more civilised way...

Milla was prepared to change direction when she had to, Tal thought. And the danger of the Selski was over.

Or was it? As the sleigh continued on, Tal noticed that the continuous drumming sound was getting louder – much, much louder. And the glow that filled the ice and sky was brighter and closer.

Tal could see more huge shapes, too, leaping and sliding. Lots and lots of them. He was just about to say something when Milla suddenly cracked her whip and shouted. The Wreska broke into an even faster gait.

The sleigh picked up speed. Tal stared at the ice in front of them, willing it to be clearer than it was. To his left he could see a solid wall of Selski travelling away from them. To his right, there was an enormous mass of Selski sliding and leaping towards them, an almost solid wall of strangely glowing flesh, preceded by a rolling wave of ice and snow.

The drumming sound was now a bass roar that drowned all other sounds.

They had begun to cross the Living Sea of the Selski, but it didn't look like the right place or the right time to Tal. The onrushing Selski were too close and the gap between the two parts of the horde was closing.

"We must take shelter at the rock!" Milla screamed, her words fighting against the noise of the Selski. She pointed to a dark mass ahead that Tal had thought was another Selski. He hadn't noticed that it wasn't moving.

He didn't think they could make it.

The rock that thrust up through the ice was only as tall as the Selski themselves and not much broader than three of them abreast. Known as the Seventy-second Splitter to the Icecarls, it was just big enough to make the Selski pass to either side rather than try to jump over it.

The sleigh pulled into the shelter of the rock just as the leading Selski crashed down behind them, closing the gap. Tal stared back in shock, barely able to believe that they'd made it. Ice chips from the Selski's landing showered over him and into his open mouth.

Tal kept looking as the ice melted on his tongue.

Huge bodies leaped and crashed, but somehow missed one another. Beyond the light of the sleigh lamps, Tal could only see the luminous patterns of the Kalikoi on the huge animals, a weaving tapestry of light that jumped and moved.

The creatures did not make any noise themselves, or if they did, it was lost in the crash and roar of so many thousands of them rising and falling upon the ice.

"What do we do now?" Tal asked finally. He had to shout close to Milla's ear.

"Climb the Splitter and look out for another gap!" Milla shouted back. She jumped down from the sleigh and started to check the Wreska's legs and their three-toed hooves, looking for strains or damage.

Tal sat down in the sleigh, pulled his hood as tight as it would go, and with his fingers on the outside, pushed the fur into his ears. Not that it helped much. The noise of the Selski's strange leaping movement vibrated through the sleigh and every bone in his body.

After ten minutes of trying to rest, Tal realised that fur stuffed into his ears didn't work. So he did what any of the Chosen would do in such a situation. He looked down at his shadowguard and said, "Shadowguard, shadowguard, shield me from sound."

The shadowguard, which was pale in the lantern light, merely twitched its copy of Tal's head in a slight sideways motion. Tal thought it hadn't heard him because of the Selski noise, so he repeated his instruction more loudly. Still nothing happened.

He was just about to shout at it, when Milla jumped back into the sleigh. Seeing Tal crouched down looking at his shadowguard, she growled and reached for her knife.

"No shadow magic!" she shouted. "You were told!"

The shadowguard didn't move. It might as well have been a natural shadow. Tal straightened up and pulled out the bits of hood that were stuck in his ears. He didn't say anything, but Milla slowly relaxed, letting her hand drift away from her knife.

"There is a gap coming!" she shouted. "We must be ready."

Tal couldn't hear every word, but he heard "gap" and got the gist of it. He turned to face forwards and gripped the rail of the sleigh. Milla moved up next to him, carefully avoiding his shadow. She drew the whip and flicked it out next to the Wreska.

Selski still leaped ahead of them, without any sign of their numbers lessening. The glow from all their Kalakoi was no less bright and the noise had not diminished.

Tal waited. When there were no Selski in sight ahead, Milla would start the Wreska, he thought. And once again they would be on their way to the Castle.

Milla cracked the whip and yelled at the Wreska while there were still Selski right in front of them. The sleigh began to move off, apparently into their path. Tal gripped the rail even harder and shouted "No!" though he couldn't even hear himself.

Then they were out of the shelter of the Splitter, crossing the churned up, split ice a scant few stretches behind the glowing, Kalakoi-riddled tail of a Selski. Tal instantly looked to the right, expecting to see one of the huge monsters in mid-air about to come crashing down on them.

But there were no Selski, at least not close.

Milla had seen a gap from atop the Splitter and

noted the Kalakoi pattern on the last Selski.

The gap was a narrow one. Once again, the Icecarl shouted at the Wreska and cracked her whip over their heads. One of the leaders stumbled, and for a terrible moment Tal thought it would go down and the sleigh would crash. But it recovered and they sped onwards across the ice.

This time, Tal felt sure that the Selski would catch them, flatten them. The sleigh would be smashed into the ice... and him with it. He drew his Sunstone, though it was too small to offer much hope. A blast of light might make one Selski turn aside, but there would be hundreds... maybe even thousands behind that one.

The sleigh hit more broken ice and rocked to one side. Tal had to let his Sunstone go in order to grab the rail with both hands and avoid being thrown out. Milla shouted something and grabbed him, her grip on his arm so strong that it was like needles of ice.

The sleigh tipped again, one runner in the air. Milla threw herself the other way, Tal going with her. For a second it looked like that would be enough, but there was another bump and the sleigh catapulted into the air and tipped on its side.

Somehow, Milla managed to keep Tal with her as the sleigh screeched and careened on its side, no longer going straight, but sliding off in a crazy arc. Wreska screamed, ice spikes flew everywhere. Tal wasn't even sure which way was up for a moment. All he could think of was the Selski bearing down on them.

Eventually, he realised the sleigh had stopped. Milla dragged him out, her knife in her hand. Tal stumbled along with her as she slashed the reins that held the Wreska to the wreckage. As soon as the traces were cut, the antlered animals bounded away. They knew the danger of the Selski, too.

"Run!" Milla screamed, shocking Tal into action. He'd been dazed without realising it. Now he came back to life. Milla was snatching the one unbroken lantern and a pack from the ruined sleigh. The Selski were so close, the ice shivering at their approach.

He started to run, but in the wrong direction. Milla pushed him towards the onrushing wave of Selski. Tal resisted, till he realised that Milla was leading the way not just towards the Selski, but to a point where their line ended.

The other side of the Living Sea. It was so close – but so were the Selski.

Milla was already ahead, not looking back. Tal sucked in cold air, feeling it burn to the bottom of his lungs, but he needed it to keep his legs going. He ran as hard as he ever had in his life.

Ahead of him, Milla stumbled and went sprawling on the ice. Without even thinking, Tal slowed and swooped down to pick her up. She was much heavier than he expected, but somehow they got up together and now they ran clutching on to each other for balance, arms windmilling to correct their slips and slides.

They could see the outermost Selski clearly now, the one they had to pass to safety. The Kalakoi had grown on it in a pattern that made it seem to have many eyes, glowing red and yellow and orange, all seemingly focused on the two tiny figures that dashed in front of the leviathan.

The Selski hit the ice and the force of its impact sent shallow cracks racing in all directions. They shot under Tal's and Milla's feet, so their run became a crazy dance to avoid tripping over a crack, which would be certain death.

The leviathan's mighty flippers pressed down on the ice again and its great bulk began to lift. Just as it shot up and forwards, Tal and Milla used all their remaining strength in a last desperate sprint that took them right in front of the straining beast. They saw its small, dark eye focus on them with surprise, and its great mouth that was always open, latticed with tiny teeth for straining Slepenish and moths.

Higher and higher it raised above them, filling the whole sky. Both of them screamed, and then they tripped and fell, sliding on backs and bellies across the ice.

The Selski leaped again and its tail came crashing down.

Tal saw it coming down and closed his eyes. Milla saw, too, but she kept her eyes open. Icecarls believed in facing death.

The tail missed them by a stretch, but they were struck with so many chunks of snow and ice that for a second Tal thought he had been hit and killed. It took a while to sink in that he was still alive.

Milla helped him up and they staggered off, the Icecarl girl leading. Selski kept thundering past behind them, but none so close.

It took them half an hour to walk far enough away to be able to talk, and for Milla to consider them safe from Selski who might be on the edges of the horde. She took off her pack and sat on it. Tal also sat, trusting his thick furs to keep the chill of the ice off his backside for a while.

"We have crossed the Living Sea," said Milla proudly, almost to herself. She didn't seem at all concerned about the loss of the sleigh and the Wreska, who had long since disappeared into the eternal night.

Something in her voice made Tal ask her a question. "You haven't crossed it before?"

"No." Milla slid off her face mask and smiled, though not at Tal particularly. "We do not cross the Living Sea except in times of direst need. They will sing a story of our crossing when I return."

"Great," said Tal bitterly. "I thought you did it all the time. I would never have agreed—"

He stopped as he saw that Milla wasn't even listening. She was completely crazy and so were all the Icecarls. The sooner he was back in the Castle the better. Even Great-uncle Ebbitt wasn't as mad as Milla.

He looked out into the darkness. The paltry light of the moths in the lantern was barely enough to see Milla's face and his shadowguard was almost invisible. Beyond that was absolute blackness. Once again, Tal had to fight a desire to lift his Sunstone up and call all the light he could.

There could be anything out there, lurking in the dark.

"You can rest for a while, then we'll go on," Milla said. "I will keep watch. It will take us longer without the sleigh."

"Obviously," grumbled Tal. He could already feel the chill of the ice coming through his furs. How was he supposed to rest?

But somehow he did fall asleep. When he awoke, feeling cold and very stiff, Milla was preparing food. She had placed a bone dish on the ice, filled with oil of some kind, and was striking sparks with two small pieces of a dull silver metal over it. After a few tries, the sparks lit the oil. Milla then took a three-legged stand of bone from her pack, set it above the burning oil and put a small pot on the stand. From the smell, Tal knew she was cooking more Selski meat.

"How do you hunt the Selski?" he asked as he got up and stamped his feet and clapped his hands to revive his circulation. The air around his chest, neck and face was surprisingly warm, and his

Sunstone felt almost hot against his chest. He must have unconsciously drawn upon its power while he was asleep. "They seem too big and too dangerous."

"We take the old and the slow," replied Milla. "On the fringes of the Living Sea. The ones that the Kalakoi have begun to eat. Even so it is dangerous and it can take twenty or thirty hunters many, many stretches to bring one to a stop."

"What happens then?" asked Tal. It was all so strange and mysterious, this world outside the Castle. A world none of the Chosen knew anything about. Or at least, Tal didn't think they did. Surely, he would have heard of the Icecarls, the Selski and the Merwin.

"They die," Milla said, with a shrug. "If the Selski stop, they die. Here, you eat first."

"Are we going to eat with the same spoon?" Tal asked, disgusted. She was so crude!

"You can go hungry instead and die," Milla snarled. Tal saw some of the old hatred flare up in her eyes. But she quickly looked away and began to spoon up chunks of warmed Selski meat.

When she was about halfway through, hunger

overcame Tal's objections. He made a tentative reach for the pot. Without speaking, Milla handed him the spoon.

That marked how they got on for the next seven days – or at least Tal *thought* it was seven days. He could tell the time in the Castle from his Sunstone, but that only gave him hours. Sometimes he lost track.

All the days were the same anyway. They walked and walked and walked, sometimes up icy hills, sometimes down, sometimes on the flat. Milla rarely spoke, except to give Tal orders. Every few hours they stopped to eat, or take turns to rest, or go to the toilet.

Toilet stops were a dangerous activity in the cold and dark. With only the one lantern, Tal had to use his Sunstone when he wandered off a little to take care of his needs, and call extra warmth from it to keep essential parts of him unfrozen. He didn't know how Milla managed. Presumably, Icecarls had their ways.

Tal was just returning from such an excursion when Milla came bounding towards him, her green moth-lamp shuttered so its light only shone in front of her.

"Hide your light!" Milla commanded. She pulled at Tal's arm to make him crouch down.

Tal quickly focused on his Sunstone, dimmed its light and slipped the chain back under his coat.

"What is it?" he whispered.

"Merwin," Milla whispered back. "A big one. It was on our trail, but I have thrown Selski meat to lure it aside. We must move away from here as quietly as we can, with as little light as possible."

Tal remembered Milla telling him back on the ship about the Merwin. It seemed like years ago.

"Hold on to my belt," Milla murmured. Tal gripped it and they started off slowly. Milla shuttered the lantern down still more, pulling the handle at its base that closed the weave. Tal could hardly see at all, but somehow it didn't bother him half as much as it would have even a few days before. He was getting used to the dark.

And, he had to admit, he'd kind of got used to Milla, since she obviously did take the blood ritual thing seriously and would do her best to get him safely to the Castle. That was a huge improvement to when she'd just wanted to kill him. Not that she was anything more than the descendant of an escaped Underfolk or something.

Milla suddenly stopped. Tal almost ran into her. They both stood there silently, in the dark. They could hear each other breathing, cold rasps coming through their masks, no matter how quiet they tried to be.

Tal could sense Milla staring out at something, but it was too dark for him to see which way she was looking. He moved his own gaze slowly, looking for anything that stood out in the darkness.

When he did see something, it took him a second to remember what it must be. A long, thin light of surprising brightness that seemed to be moving by itself, slowly meandering from side to side.

A Merwin's horn.

The glowing horn, three times as long as Tal, slowly came closer and closer. Tal felt rather than saw Milla draw her knife. Her spears had been broken in the crash of the sleigh.

A short piece of sharpened bone did not seem like much of a weapon against a hunting beast with a horn that could ram through Tal and Milla and still have plenty left over.

Slowly, trying to make the movement as hidden as he could, Tal reached into his coat and began to pull out his Sunstone.

He had it half out when the Merwin finally worked out where they were. A terrible whistling screech filled the air and the luminous horn suddenly rocketed forwards.

Milla shouted something and pushed Tal away. She ran, too, but forwards, towards the Merwin. Tal could see it clearly now, illuminated by its own terrible horn.

The picture he saw then would be etched in his mind forever.

The Merwin was even bigger than Milla's description – at least twenty stretches long. It looked like a Kralsnake from the Beastmaker game, all thin and sinewy. Except it had four long, clawed flippers instead of legs and shiny black hide instead of scales.

It had only one eye – a huge golden eye, long and slitted, with a lid that kept flicking open and shut several times a second. The other side of its narrow head showed an empty, scarred eye socket, clearly a wound from long ago.

The horn grew from a ridge of bone between the Merwin's eyes. Under it was the creature's mouth, big enough, with its many shining teeth, to eat Tal in a single gulp.

As Milla charged towards it, the terrible horn struck. It came straight at the Icecarl and for an instant Tal thought it would go right through her.

But she dodged and almost got past. The Merwin flicked its head and the ferociously sharp point of the horn sliced across her chest, the force of it throwing her to the ice. She did not get up.

The Merwin hesitated. It started to move towards the motionless body of Milla, its horn scraping the ice. Once again, Milla's words went through Tal's brain.

"...*they stick their horn through whatever they're after and then they bash it up and down on the ice...*"

The Merwin reared back to strike at the defenceless girl.

"No!" Tal screamed. He rushed forwards with his Sunstone raised in his hand.

Faster than Tal's eye could catch, the Merwin changed targets. It lunged forwards, extending its body, the luminous horn coming straight at Tal. He threw himself to one side and would have fallen, but his shadowguard was there to prop him up.

Somehow he also managed to keep his Sunstone trained on the creature's one golden eye.

Tal knew he would only have time for a single blast of light before the sharp horn struck again. He focused all his thought on the Sunstone, drawing upon every fragment of power it possessed – and unleashed it at the Merwin.

The flash was so bright that Tal was blinded. The Merwin shrieked, an awful, high-pitched sound that seemed all too close, but Tal didn't know whether he'd just annoyed it or burned out its one remaining eye.

He cursed himself for being so stupid and not closing his own eyes. He could hear the Merwin thrashing around and could imagine that horn stabbing towards him. He started to run, then stopped, disoriented. Maybe he was running towards the Merwin!

"Shadowguard!" he called and he held out his hand. Something tingling and soft touched his fingers and jerked him to one side. Tal fell and felt the swish of air as something passed him, followed immediately by the sound of the Merwin's horn striking the ice.

Either it could still see or its other senses were good enough to find him. Tal rolled aside, then crawled as his shadowguard pulled at his hand. His sight was slowly coming back, the darkness becoming a mixture of floating blobs and fuzzy light.

The Merwin struck again, its horn skittering off the ice near Tal's feet. He turned to face it, his vision coming clear again. It was blind, at least temporarily, its golden eye closed and weeping. But it could hear or smell, or sense, for its head was pointed straight at him, as was the horn.

It would eventually get him, unless Tal did something first. But his Sunstone was finished, completely used up, and his shadowguard could not fight something like this.

Even if he did somehow manage to get away, he would be lost in the dark, without a light of any kind. Without light, his shadowguard would dissipate. Without the shadowguard, he had no way of finding the Castle.

Perhaps he could get Milla's lantern and knife. Tal started to edge around, back towards the faint green glow where Milla had fallen. He was surprised to see that his blind escape from the Merwin had taken him so far from her body.

He was even more surprised when Milla suddenly leaped out of the darkness, on to the Merwin's neck. She wrapped her legs round it, locked her ankles together and plunged her dagger deep into its head.

The Merwin screeched and reared up, its bright horn pointing directly at the sky. Milla stabbed it again and it flung its head back down, smashing her legs into the ice. But she hung on and stabbed it again and again, despite its writhings and desperate banging against the ice.

Finally, it stopped moving and the light from its horn began to dim. Milla let go and crawled a short distance away. Tal could see the blood on her fur and trails of Merwin ichor upon the ice.

Tal gulped. He had stood mesmerised while Milla fought the creature. Now he ran forwards.

Milla lay on her back. Her hood had fallen down and her mask was nowhere to be seen. In the fading light of the Merwin's horn, Tal saw that her face was even whiter and her lips were turning blue. The whole front of her coat was ripped to shreds and her fur leggings were rent in many places. As Tal watched, blood began to pool beneath her. Dark red blood, not the blue ichor of the Merwin.

"I die," said Milla, her voice soft. Clumsily, she wiped her wrist across her chest and held it up, all bloody to Tal. "By this blood that we share, blood of the Clan, bone of the ship, the Quest must..."

Her voice trailed off and she seemed to see something that confused her. Her forehead furrowed, then her eyes slowly closed.

For a moment, Tal thought that she was dead. But as he kneeled by her side, he saw that she still breathed, though shallowly.

Taking great care, Tal peeled back her torn furs. He had to force himself to take slow breaths as he saw the wound that stretched across her left side. Having seen it, he didn't know what to do. His Sunstone was dead and even if it wasn't, he didn't know enough to use it for healing.

Then he felt a soft touch at his arm. His shadowguard was plucking at his wrist, the wrist marked with the three cuts of the Icecarls.

Tal stared at the shadow. It was trying to tell him something. It had taken a shape he didn't recognise. Something human.

Then it hit him. The shadowguard had assumed the shape of Milla's shadow. It was saying that since she had some of his blood, it could help her. All Tal had to do was tell it to.

"Shadowguard, shadowguard," he blurted out. "Staunch Milla's wounds—"

Before he could finish, the shadowguard flowed over Milla. Most of it stuck to her ribs, but dark tendrils rippled down to her legs and out along her left arm. Wherever it touched, the bleeding stopped.

Tal pulled Milla's furs together over both girl and shadowguard. He retrieved the pack and lantern. It took him a moment to work out how to open it up again, then he sat it down next to Milla. The shadowguard would need all the light it could get.

Even once the bleeding stopped, Tal wasn't sure if Milla would survive. Now that he had a chance to think, he wasn't even sure he wanted her to. She had probably saved his life, but now he had the pack and the lantern. He might be better off heading straight for the Castle. He certainly didn't want to be bothered with trying to get her a Sunstone as well.

It wasn't as if she was family or a friend or anything.

What would his parents say, Tal suddenly thought. What would his father do if he was out here? Or his mother, if she were well?

They wouldn't leave her. Only someone like Shadowmaster Sushin would and Tal did not want to be like him.

He sighed and opened the pack. First, he got out a sleeping fur, which he carefully tucked round the unconscious girl, tilting her up to get it between her back and the ice. Then he set up the oil burner and began to heat some Selski broth. He supposed Milla would need something hot when she came to.

"What's happening to me?" he asked the dead carcass of the Merwin as the broth bubbled. "I am Tal Graile-Rerem of the Chosen. I'm not supposed to be sitting in the middle of nowhere looking after a... a mad Icecarl girl. I should be back home, with a new Sunstone, getting ready for the Day of Ascension."

The dead Merwin did not answer. But someone else did.

"And where exactly is your home?" said a voice out in the darkness, beyond the diminishing glow of the Merwin's horn. A woman's voice that sounded rather like the Crone of the Far-Raiders.

Tal jumped and scrabbled madly for Milla's knife. By the time he found it and held it out, the speaker was already at his side. She had a spear at his throat.

She was not alone.

A ring of Icecarls stood around Tal, Milla and the dead Merwin. There were at least twelve of them and they all had spears levelled, as if Tal was as dangerous as the creature Milla had killed.

He had not heard them approach. They might as well have blown in on the wind or sprouted up from the ice.

They wore different-coloured furs than the Far-Raiders, and their masks were decorated with wavy lines that glowed like the Kalakoi on the Selski. Clearly, they were from a different Clan. He hoped killing the Merwin didn't count as thieving on their hunting lands. Then again, Milla had tried to kill him just for being there…

"I am a Chosen of the Castle," he said slowly. "But I am on a Quest with Milla there, of the Far-Raiders. I am bound to the Clan and to the ship. Look!"

He held up his wrist and peeled his gauntlet back to show the marks on his wrist.

"You have no shadow," said the woman who had spoken. "Where is it?"

"Helping Milla," Tal said anxiously. Now he knew what Icecarls were really like, he didn't want to give them an excuse to kill him. "The Merwin hurt her. My shadow has just stopped the bleeding, that's all."

The woman looked down at Milla and pulled the

fur aside. She still kept her spear pointed at Tal.

"Tell me how you came here from your Castle and how you met the Far-Raiders," the woman commanded.

Tal told her, the words practically falling out of his mouth. This lot of Icecarls was even scarier than Milla. The ones standing around hadn't moved at all. They just stood there, with their sharp spears glinting.

As Tal told his story, he surreptitiously looked at the Icecarls. Not only were their furs and masks different from the Far-Raiders', he noticed they were all wearing exactly the same clothes, not at all like the Icecarls he'd met before. He had almost reached the part about the Merwin when he suddenly realised who they must be. They had to be Shield Maidens, the sisterhood that Milla wanted to join. They were like completely grown-up Millas, which was a really frightening thought.

He finished the story. The first woman stood in silence, towering above him. She started to raise her spear and Tal gulped. Surely, he couldn't have come this far only to be stabbed to death because a mad Shield Maiden didn't believe his story!

"Breg, Libbe, Umen – see to the girl," said the woman. "You. Tal. You will come with us."

"Where?" asked Tal. "And... is it all right for me to ask who you are?"

"I am Arla, Shield Mother," replied the woman. "We are Shield Maidens, currently serving the Mother Crone of the Mountain of Light."

"The Mountain of Light?" asked Tal eagerly. That was what the Far-Raiders' Crone had called the mountain the Castle was built upon. "Are we near to it?"

"Three sleeps," replied Arla. "You will soon see it in the sky."

"I'm going home!" exclaimed Tal. He jumped up, but stopped as several Shield Maidens thrust their spears out at him.

"You are a prisoner. We will take you to our Crone for judgement," Arla explained. "It is forbidden to climb the Mountain of Light and I am not sure you have told the truth. If you or your shadow try to escape, or do magic, you will be killed. Do you understand?"

"Yes," said Tal. He felt very tired all of a sudden. Every time it seemed he might get back to the Castle without further difficulties, something happened.

"We have a sleigh," said Arla. "You can ride on it with your Clan-bond, Milla."

Tal remembered very little of the journey to the Shield Maidens' headquarters in the foothills of the Mountain of Light. Their sleigh was much bigger than Milla's, drawn by twelve Wreska. But it was built for cargo and so was slower and uncomfortable. Tal and Milla were wedged between Selski-skin sacks containing something that smelled absolutely putrid.

Milla had only brief moments of consciousness and said little that made any sense. Tal wasn't entirely sure he spent much of the journey conscious either. He slept or half slept most of the way, his dreams and recent events merging. He was stalked by Sharrakor, who became a one-eyed Merwin. He climbed a mast and found his father and Ebbitt perched there, drinking sweetwater.

Again and again, he dreamed of his fall from the Red Tower and of Sunstones. Sunstones falling all around him, just out of reach.

One thing he did remember and was sure was not a dream. That was his first sight of what the Icecarls called the Mountain of Light.

Woken by a strange chanting, he had looked over the side of the sleigh to see all the Shield Maidens lined up, facing in one direction, chanting something softly together. He had followed their gaze and had seen it.

The Castle. Far, far off and high up, but like a flower of light in the sky, a flower of a thousand brilliant petals. It seemed to hang there, the mountain invisible in the darkness beneath.

Home, thought Tal. *Home*.

Now he could see it, he knew he would return. The Shield Mother's Crone would see that he spoke the truth, like the one on the ship. She would let him continue his Quest. She had to.

He looked down at Milla, who was lying still amid the sacks. His shadowguard had been replaced by bandages and poultices made with herbs and creams Tal didn't know.

Her hand was lying outside the furs, the three

cuts on her wrist clearly visible. Tal looked at his own wrist, the healing scars quite bright in the green light of the moth-lamps.

Then he looked at her shadow. Somehow it didn't seem quite the same as the Underfolk's natural shadows. The Icecarls were different, Tal had decided. They weren't Chosen, but they certainly weren't servants.

"I will bring you to the Castle," Tal said. He bent down and touched his wrist to Milla's. "And we will both get Sunstones."

The next thing Tal knew, Milla's hand was at his throat and she was staring at him wild-eyed and feverish. Despite her weakness, he only just managed to wrench her hand free and stagger to the other side of the sleigh.

"Why won't it die?" she asked. She shook her head from side to side, then collapsed back on to the furs.

"We're on our way to the Castle," croaked Tal, massaging his neck. He wished he hadn't said anything, because he already wanted to change his mind about taking Milla.

He could not believe how far he'd come and how

far he had to go. Despite battle-crazy Icecarls, hostile Spiritshadows, gigantic Merwin and the freezing cold, he had somehow made it through these unknown lands. Could he possibly be the same boy who'd lived all his days in the Castle – all his days not knowing what existed outside?

No, he was not the same. He would never be the same again.

Of course, after he convinced the Crone to let them go, they would still have to climb the mountain. Then there was the question of how to get into the Castle itself. Having never left it – at least not on the ground – Tal had no idea how it was done.

All he knew was that somehow he would do it.

Tal was going home.

Coming soon, book two of

THE SEVENTH TOWER

CASTLE

Turn over for a sneak preview...

Tal looked down at the gap again. It would be suicide to try and jump over it. He couldn't even see the bottom. They were almost at a turn in the road, so it would be a straight drop to the road below. That had to be at least five hundred stretches!

He looked back. Milla was strapping the toothy jawbones they used as spikes on to her boots. She had also taken out something Tal hadn't seen before. Gloves of thin Selski hide with long curved claws of reddish bone.

"You will have to help me with the claw-hands," Milla said as she finished strapping on her boot-teeth. She then tried to hammer a bone piton into the road, but it wouldn't go through the sections where there was metal and the stone crumbled everywhere else.

Finally, Milla shrugged and put the piton back. She left her pack lying on the ground and strapped her Merwin-horn sword on to her back instead. She slipped on the clawed gloves. Tal saw that they had to tied on to her wrists, so he helped her, patiently following her instructions on how to do the right knots.

"Move the lanterns to the edge," said Milla. She

had not put her mask back on. Tal saw her eyes move calculatingly to the far edge.

"Shouldn't you be tied to a rope?" he asked. "I could hold it…"

"There is nothing to secure it to," said Milla. "You would only be dragged down."

She hesitated, then said, "If I fail, Tal, you will try to go on? You will fulfil the Quest and get a Sunstone for my clan? Then I may become a Shield Maiden, even after death."

Tal looked at the dark gap and was tempted to say that if Milla couldn't jump it, he would have no chance. But she had used his name and hadn't looked at him with her usual scorn. "I will try," he said, with a gulp.

"I would not ask normally," said Milla. "But I am still not at my full strength."

"Great," Tal muttered under his breath. He looked at the gap again, then reached out to touch Milla's claw-hands.

"All right, I'll jump first," he said.

"What?" Milla was suddenly angry again. "Do you doubt my courage?"

She took her hands away and stalked back twenty or so steps, out of the light of the lanterns.

"I'll show you a Shield Maiden's courage!" she shouted angrily.

"No, Milla!" shouted Tal. "Wait! I didn't mean... take your time—"

Before he could finish, Milla came sprinting out of the darkness. She passed Tal in a blur, her arms and legs pumping. Two paces from the edge, she threw herself forwards, arms outstretched.

"Yaaaahhhhhhhh!"

Tal rushed to the edge. There was a clatter of rocks. He couldn't see Milla on the other side. He raised one of the lanterns, a sick feeling in his stomach.

Nothing moved in the small pool of light.

"Milla!" Tal shouted, his voice echoing into the emptiness.